Shear

SHEAR

Tim Parks

Grove Press
New York

First published in Great Britain in 1993 by William Heinemann Ltd.
First Grove Press edition, July 1994

Printed in the United States of America

FIRST EDITION

Library of Congress Cataloging-in-Publication Data
Park, Tim.
Shear / Tim Parks.—1st Grove Press ed., 1st ed.
ISBN 0-8021-1552-7
I. Title.
PR6066.A6957S54   1994   823'.914—dc20   94-7058

Grove Press
841 Broadway
New York, NY 10003

10 9 8 7 6 5 4 3 2 1

'The mortal cannot go fearless through these many-coloured beauties.'

Aeschylus, *Agamemnon*, 923–4

AUTHOR'S NOTE

I suppose it was bound to occur to me, during the months of writing *Shear*, that the way a novel comes into being is not so unlike the way some rocks form. Sediments are brought to us downriver, through our experience, over the air waves, the books we read. Some roll on by, others are deposited on the bedding plane of our own particular mental tilt, where, once captured, there will be the cement of our conditioning and prejudices, the more conscious pressure of what might be called vision, or is more likely just the desperation to make what sense we can. And under that pressure these disparate sediments are gradually aligned, they crystallize, become a recognisable mass, a rock different from every other rock. For no two rocks are ever quite the same.

In the case of *Shear* the nature of those sediments was all too plain. There were the years of work for the Italian quarrying industry, a huge burden of geological/mechanical vocabulary that was bound to shape the terrain of some novel or other. There was the intense pleasure I was finding in translating Roberto Calasso's splendid book on the classical world, *The Marriage of Cadmus and Harmony*. Less happily, there were the upheavals that were destroying and remaking the lives of people close to me. What formed from the collision of these unlikely elements would gradually come to have the structure of an adventure, the colour of a love story, the brittle lustre of a defeat. And if in thin section over bright light individual samples of this mass are found to have the same pattern, then that must be the pressure of what was intended as a meditation on the notion of the unique: in life, in the things we make, in love.

Naturally I soon became endeared to my little analogy, partly because I had thought of it myself, and partly because it seemed to me to accommodate the arbitrary in a way romantic descriptions of the 'artwork' as naturally growing into its necessary shape do not. It also has the advantage of rejecting the pretence of classicists that a writer is in complete control of his book, or could have planned the final structure from the beginning. And if, which I'm not sure of, writing a good novel is more difficult today than once it was, then this may be because the sediments we find rolling downriver to us are more numerous and heterogeneous than in the past, come from further afield, and are rarely in equilibrium with their new environment. So that a great deal more pressure, and perhaps a good deal of heat too, will be necessary to have them lie down together, metamorphose, fuse, crystallize. And the more violent the process, the greater, one imagines, will be the danger of discontinuities, the propensity to, as one ignores to one's peril, shear.

Day Two

That night he dreamt there was evil in the rock. So, such concepts still exist in dreams, was his first thought on waking, and careful not to disturb, he got up to write his report, for the room was full of light. Ancient concepts, though not so old as the rock he had placed them in. The men had sunk their boreholes, fed in the penthrite. The air was gritty with a dust of feldspar from the last of the drill steels pushed hot on to its rack. Quartz glittered about their boots, then frothed to mud as the holes were stemmed. The water bubbled out. They retreated. Until, as hand reached for plunger, he suddenly became aware that there was evil in the rock. Not that the material was poor or excessively faulted. But there was evil there. There were unforeseeable consequences. Nesting in amongst the crystals, potent as the forces that had fashioned the landscape. His chest was tight and he couldn't speak. He opened his mouth soundlessly. His fingers clawed. And inevitably the blast woke him.

Tapping on a portable keyboard on the kind of rickety desk they will provide in such places, he wrote:

'The material in question is classifiable as late tectonic plutonite belonging to the group of leucocratic, fine-grained, equal-grained monzogranites. For the Talava pluton, the isochrynous line determined by the Rb/Sr method on total rock points to an age of 275 ± 4 MY.'

Two hundred and seventy-five million years.

He stopped, and, looking up, caught a glimpse of her in the uncertain silvering of a cheap wardrobe mirror. She was twenty-two.

It was seven thirty-five. European summertime.

And he wrote:

'Despite the brevity of the visit, some negative aspects of the local geological situation at Palinu quarry were immediately evident. The surface layer of weathered material is remarkably thick, 5 to 8 metres, and its removal is achieved with explosives (see plate 3). In the underlying mass . . .'

There had been no weathered material on Margaret. The writer stopped and thought about this. Rather, her explosion had blown off the weathered crust on him, taken both of them to a primitive state of fused magma. He closed his eyes. For some minutes it was as if he were in trance, outside time. Then he went back to the liquid-crystal ciphers on the desk before him.

'In the underlying mass there are many fractures (see plate 2) following principal and secondary planes which intersect and determine quite severe rock discontinuities.'

There came a knock on the door.

It was repeated and a low voice called, 'Mr Nicholson. Mr Nicholson, please.'

It was a voice he both knew and didn't know. An accent. Was Margaret still asleep? He went to the door and, turning the key, found the dead man's wife in front of him.

'Mr Nicholson, I know it's early, I'm sorry, but I'd like to talk to you. I thought maybe we could have breakfast together.'

For a moment he experienced the same vocal paralysis he had had in his dream. Basically he was annoyed. The Australian woman shifted her weight from one foot to the other. Smaller than himself. Not quite chubby.

'Ten minutes,' he told her, making sure she could not see into the room.

Margaret slept. He sat beside her and drew back the sheet a little. The colour in daylight was white to pink, perhaps potassium–aluminium silicate, but with a pearly lustre. Which was appropriate. Pearly Margaret, not a stone, but very precious. And what impurity could have made the hair so red? What impurity! Smirking, he took a quick shower and left a note on the desk: 'You'll need all the sleep you can get!'

———— • ————

Mrs Owen was apologising. She had her little girl with her now, as on the previous afternoon. And she was sorry she had come so early, but she was afraid he might already be off at work, as he had been yesterday. She needed to see him on his own.

'You came to my room yesterday?' he asked too quickly. Then he shifted his gaze to where the window offered a first-floor view across the square: porphyry cobbles in interlocking fans, travertine sills and plinths, marble the little statue perhaps, the fountain basin – and above, between, around those stones, the people in their cars, their different dimension. Slim legs scissored off the corner of his field of vision to the right. The light was so bright here.

'You see, I want to find out who was responsible for my husband's death. I want to make them pay for it.'

He was torn between the need to be kind and wise and the desire to get back to his room for what he hoped might be enjoyed before the day's work began. Then he saw that her girl was smoothing the hair of a Little Pony identical to his own daughter's. And he said, 'Haranguing a quarry foreman won't help. You could have got yourself killed.

In fact, to be frank, I can't really see why you're here at all.'

'They're winning that rock the wrong way,' she said. There was more than a hint of belligerence.

'How do you mean?'

'The explosives.'

'About ninety per cent of the world's granite is won with explosives.'

'But they're using too much. They're being careless, to make more money. I read it in a report.'

'There are definitely some problems,' he conceded.

The waiter came to stand beside their table. Neither of them could speak his language. In many ways they were like particles transported here from some overburden far away, not easily assimilable. Or not at this temperature. The mother persuaded her girl that you did not eat ice-cream in the morning. Cake proved a sufficiently international word. Coffee was no problem at all.

Then Mrs Owen said, look, she believed in God. She believed there was right and wrong and people had got to recognise that and accept responsibility. Right? Otherwise civilisation stank. Otherwise it was merely a question of making money and the devil take the hindmost.

He was embarrassed, watching as she rummaged in her handbag. The way all women do. An animal burrowing. To produce a photograph in which a forty-year-old man simply smiled into a camera at close quarters against a domestic background. There was a chip on one front tooth. But nothing unusual about it. He could hardly have imagined anything else. What worried him was that the girl might be upset. But she was having her Little Pony nuzzle in the cream of her cake now with healthy unconcern.

'He had protested about the safety standards. He was worried about the speed his men were being asked to work at. He said there was something wrong with the rock. He had found reports. Then one morning they phone me to say . . .'

Tears brimmed in her eyes. Handing back the photo, the geologist slopped some coffee, and noticed that the green table-top was a plastic imitation of serpentine, complete with swirling, conchoidal cleavage. They were getting so clever at that kind of thing. Mrs Owen's own cleavage became evident for a moment as she reached down and sideways for her bag again, her handkerchiefs. The curves were neither round nor full. He drained his coffee and waited patiently. The little girl began to nag for more cake. Her mother told her quite sharply to sit still.

She said, 'The thing is, you're an expert, Mr Nicholson. You could tell me who was responsible. Or help me to find out. There are papers I can give you. That's all I need. Then I'll decide what to do about it.'

———— • ————

Margaret was in the shower. He grabbed his bag and jacket. But then wanted at least to see her. She hadn't locked, so he was able to walk in and gaze through a plastic made to imitate frosted glass this time.

'Did somebody come to the room yesterday morning?' he called.

The splashing stopped. She turned off the tap, pulled in a towel and slid back the door. Margaret. She was salmon pink now. Cinnabar almost. He had never felt like this. So that he wondered if he would ever have the courage to ask for all he was learning to want.

'Someone knocked four or five times.'

'Don't open. It's a semi-psycho case. Her husband was killed in an accident and she's on some kind of crusade to make everybody pay. She almost scratched a quarryman's eyes out yesterday. Walked right up to the face just as they were about to blast it.'

He was grinning foolishly, but Margaret's face showed concern.

'You'll get your jacket wet,' she said. But he embraced her anyway. And what he liked to do was whisper sweet lewdnesses in her ear. She smiled serenely. 'All in good time. Don't forget your bag.'

In the lobby, he was aware he ought to ask if there had been a fax for him. Yes, that was the worry, the slowly cementing unpleasantness in the back of his mind. Quite probably it was that that had given him his nightmare. Evil in the rock. What could it mean? But heading for the desk, Mrs Owen was there again. Much as he sympathised, he changed direction and walked straight over to his driver at the door.

Who spoke no English. For which he was rather grateful. He watched the landscape. Steep slopes. Sparse vegetation on thin soils. Erosion of an old uplift. Much the same as might be said of his marriage, amidst the general drift of the continents. But the light was so bright here. He closed his eyes and let it glow through the blood of his eyelids. Redder than her hair. Looking into the light was the sweetest thing. He couldn't remember where he had heard that. And he opened his bag to glance quickly through his notes.

They had a beautiful woman waiting at the gate. That was the first indication somebody had over-estimated his importance. A truly beautiful woman: graphite-black hair, quick, perfectly-moulded face. And, if there comes a time in many men's lives when for sanity's sake they must decide between the escapes of total commitment to work, or having the occasional adventure, Peter Nicholson had now definitely plumped for the latter. Pandora's box was officially open. So that he even managed to consider for a moment whether bringing the wonderful Margaret mightn't have been a mistake, cramped his style. He felt extremely cheerful and happy. Runny as lava. And he said the first thing he needed to see was the deposit yard.

She clicked along beside him on heels, brushed him with airy clothes, and since her English appeared to be very good, he remarked that one of the things that had most worried him on his visit to the quarry yesterday was the poor segregation between freshly-won, rejected, or weathered material, and that awaiting slabbing. Though what he was actually looking for as he moved down the long lines of blocks in the yard was just one example of their having arrowed the direction of crystallisation wrongly. That on its own would be telling. He stopped and brushed away dust from the groove a borehole had left: a grey, subvitreous, speckled surface. The bottom line was, he said, that if a slab broke and fell off, it could kill somebody. It had killed somebody. There were insurance costs.

She was well-mannered, polite and efficient. She squatted down and explained the code roughly painted in the corner of a block. He thought he had never been shown around a granite deposit by a woman before, and said that the different destination codes suggested the company was supplying at least three projects at the same time. Whereas they had promised priority would be given to Marlborough Place.

She smiled very brightly, then actually laughed. He had always been impressed by big, white, even teeth. By health really. Though there was a poignancy in chips and discolorations. Margaret had a canine buckled over an incisor. And he remembered the chip on the dead man's tooth. Not unlike his own. But on the lower set. There was always something different about another man's blemish. Whereas the teeth now smiling at him might have been hard, paste porcelain, the original cast the race had strayed from. 'Priority does not mean exclusivity,' she smiled. He could already see her in bed. Which, of course, was a facility Margaret had given him.

Did love mean exclusivity?

Then while they stood watching the men harnessing up a block to be trolleyed into the plant, she asked him if he had come alone, or brought his wife so as to take the opportunity of having a holiday. There were so many fine beaches. And this was presumptuous, he thought, since he wore no ring. Unless it was a request for just that information, his marital status. Peter hesitated. A distant explosion sent a crowd of birds wheeling and crying from the derrick arm. The huge block inched off the ground and swung very slightly towards them, centring to gravity under the derrick. Because Dr Maifredi, she said, would be very happy to invite him to his villa, perhaps tomorrow if he was free. She would be on hand to interpret if that should be necessary, though Dr Maifredi spoke good English. There was a swimming pool. Splendid views.

And this, he thought, was the second indication. He asked his guide her name and she was called Thea.

They went on into the finishing plant, picking up headsets and overalls at the door. Here the 275-million-year-old blocks, each a vast and unique complex of quartz, feldspar, biotite mica, and a whole range of minor contributors crystallised in never-ending combinations, were to be transformed into so many identical polished slabs.

Almost immediately he began to feel ill. Most of the noise was coming from the twenty gangsaws lined up where one whole side of the plant was open to the deposit yard. On each saw a block of about four or five tons was being attacked by a heavy frame holding perhaps eighty steel blades and fed with a mixture of water, lime and cast-iron shot. Despite his headset, the incessant screaming of quartz against tempered steel and spiky shot knifed straight through his brain in a way it could not through the granite. The advance speed must be around seven or eight centimetres per hour. And all the meanwhile the big wheels forced the connecting rods back and forth, dragging and pushing their shrieking bladeframes with hypnotic plangency. He felt drawn to such things. Despite the oppressive machine clamour. The attraction was part of his feeling ill. So that now he had a fleeting image of the big blades slabbing his own body, or that of somebody precious to him. Logically, if there was evil in the rock, it was here it must be released.

Thea caught his grimace and smiled. When he nodded, she led the way to the foreman's sound-proof cabin where he asked what kind of tolerances the saws were operating to, the granulometry of the shot. Thea translated. Had it been explained to everybody how important respect of tolerance was on this job? The man was wiry, moustached, unimpressed. He kept slipping a thin bracelet on and off one dark hand, as though in mesmerised time to the slow screaming of the machine immediately outside. Even in here they had to shout; and the foreman said that final tolerance was the job of calibration and polishing, down the line. He just had to make sure the slabs weren't too thin. If they were, he switched them to the tile production line.

Despite the sprinklers and suction filters, dust was everywhere. On coming out of the cabin after the swaying back of his guide, Peter felt more sick and oppressed than before. He got the same thing visiting shale crushers. The shrieking was in his mind, the massacring reduction of stone to something willed. Thea on the contrary, seemed admirably composed.

They walked further along the gangsaws. The air was wet and grey. The connecting rods drove back and forth. The blades sank parallel. Until she stopped at a saw offloading. He pulled out a steel calibrator and measured widths as the mechanical arm lowered the slabs. A watching operative was the first black he had seen in the country. And he had to force himself to concentrate.

An hour passed. They followed through, along the line of disc trimmers and honers, as the rocks made their slow progress to the desired uniformity. At every stage, despite the pounding in his head, he measured. He told Thea to tell a worker to reject a piece 0.5 mm too thin. Eyebrows were raised. He stood by the drilling frame. The slabs were 25 millimetres thick. The holes must be 8 millimetres in diameter. Leaving throats only 8.5 millimetres each side. It wouldn't be difficult to find something to reject here. A cracked phenocryst right on the edge. The operative was impassive, made no objection. There was no question of talking. And by the first of the polishers the fumes of stannous oxide almost had him vomiting. The grinding heads skated slow circles across the stone. A tenuous lustre came up as water and paste sluiced over the slabs. Thea touched his hand and led him to the finished stacks.

He pulled out a magnifying glass to stare at what only a month ago had been deep in the palaeozoic earth. Grey Pearl it was called, a mottled play of black, white and off-white crystals, a sort of monochrome kaleidoscope in which his practised eye found two varieties of feldspar and biotite, the dominant quartz, the fine clays, surprisingly large phenocrysts, no preferred orientation, so that every square inch was still triumphantly unique despite all the long rows of machines. Indeed, they bought it for that. Modular and unrepeatable.

He asked to have a slab taken out into the sunlight and hosed down. Which two men duly did, leaning it against a derrick leg. Coming outside with them, he immediately experienced a sense of liberation. He removed his headset and breathed. And, looking obliquely across the surface of the rock, there they were: moderately aligned, originating in the quartz crystals, but spreading wide. 'Those will be twice as thick by the time it gets to Australia,' he told his guide to tell the men. 'Chuck it.'

———————— • ————————

'Imagine a man released from the pressure cooker of home for a week. His heart expands, doesn't it, his mind opens. Like a sponge when you let go. Well, it's the same with the rock when you pull it out from under the hill and slice it up. Stress relief. And as it expands, it fractures, in a cobweb of tiny cracks. Resistance to shear is reduced, it becomes more fragile.'

'I should take you straight back home then,' she had said. 'To where you're safe.'

He laughed. 'No, just don't subject me to any shear.'

'Which was?'

When pressure was applied in at least two different and not diametrically opposite directions. Wind and gravity, for example, in the case of a thin slab taken half-way around the world and carelessly hung thirty floors above a Sydney thoroughfare. In his own case it might be libido and loyalty, kids and work. Barely had he said this than they were kissing deeply. Crystal tears in her eyes.

That had been day one.

———————— • ————————

'This woman again, she was at my office this morning.' The quarry manager was a small, squat, jolly man, paunch pressed against the table, tackling meat. 'She wants it to be my fault her husband is dead.'

Peter had told Margaret he would do his best to be back for lunch. His duties were only limited. The whole visit was little more than a stunt for claims the Australian contractor was planning to make against his supplier. But now Thea was sitting next to him. Despite her formal polish, he wondered if he noticed hints of complicity beneath the surface of a smile, and if so, how big and deep that deposit might be, what means might be required to win it. A light knee touched his own.

'At first I have thought the lady comes with you,' the quarry manager went on. There was the finishing plant manager too, but he spoke no English.

'No, you're joking. Never travel with a woman.' Peter laughed. He was enjoying himself and at the same time registering the background discomfort of not knowing quite what he wanted, nor even what he should want. Only that it was exciting. There was another worry niggling too, if only he could place it. Asking the way to the loo, he found a pay phone in the cloakroom, worked out how to use it, called the hotel and asked for 221. But of course he had told her not to answer. Annoyingly, reception didn't take back the line, so he had to call again to ask if there had been a fax.

'All faxes are carried directly up to the rooms, sir.'

This had honestly not occurred to him. He stood for a moment in the booth, noticing a ceramic floor beneath his feet which admirably mimicked the polished rock he had inspected this morning. And he could presumably phone his wife direct from here. If he had had enough change. Or the desire to go and get it. For a moment he saw the phone and all its possibilities divide like a million fracture lines, a net, a web of necessity, all the way across the crumpled hills of Europe back home. Though home, at this distance, became a somewhat arbitrary notion. One house in one street. Where his children were. He decided to enjoy himself.

They were chattering in their own language. He sat down. Through the interpreter, the finishing plant manager began to enthuse about new technology and what it had meant for this particular locality. He watched the beautiful woman's lips form the words, virgin territory. 'Yes, the whole area, until just a short time ago.' And as on two or three occasions already this morning, he was aware of vague parallels with his own life. His mind seemed so alive, as though heated to a fluid state where everything might be everything else. An intense metamorphism. 'With diamond tools,' Thea parroted, 'and modern robotics, these hills can become absolutely anything: kitchen surfaces, table-tops, spiral stairs, washbowls, window surrounds, skirting elements, tiled floors and walls, bar furniture, building façades, anything.'

The finishing plant manager grinned proudly between the wineglasses. He was hang-jawed, Mediterranean. 'Is beautiful stone, no? Beautiful.'

'The only traditional use,' offered the quarry manager, 'before we can mass-produce it, was tombstones.'

Peter nodded. Then everybody caught the unfortunate allusion at exactly the same time. Like the shadow a crane casts as it swings across deposit yard or construction site, winching a heavy slab. The slab. Thea had a glass of red wine at her lips, her face almost too symmetrical. Whereas the dead man's creased photo had shown the chipped tooth, lop-sided nose, a banal uniqueness.

'But what I can't understand,' said the quarryman, 'is why the wife comes all the way here to complain. We are all very sorry of course, but . . .'

The finishing plant manager wanted to know exactly how it had happened. He hadn't even heard of the business until today. 'That is not why you are here, is it?' Thea translated the tail end of his question. Her whole left leg was lightly against his. Though this was perhaps justified by the small table.

'No, no. Not at all.' Peter was offhand. All he knew, as far as the accident was concerned, was hearsay. The man had apparently been on the scaffolding, conducting the cladding installation. The crane had come over with one of the prefab spandrel panels bearing three slabs. Something had happened. Perhaps the panel had knocked against the core structure, perhaps not. The crane operator said not. Which he would. Only half of a slab had fallen.

Very pertinently the quarry manager asked, 'How long for have they had to halt the cladding?'

Peter said he didn't know. And he repeated that his was just a routine inspection. 'The drilling is a worry. The throat width is critical, especially given the size of those phenocrysts.'

But for some reason Thea didn't bother to translate this for the man responsible.

———— • ————

The brochure they had given him with his air ticket explained that these were the islands of classical myth. Zeus had betrayed Hera with a variety of nymphs. Or Jupiter, Juno. There had been metamorphoses, the wildest sex. So the theory of uniformitarianism, Peter chuckled, held good in more fields than one. If it has happened before, it must be happening now: the geosyncline laying down its slow deposits beyond this shimmering beach, that girl who compelled you to look. The one awaiting the unimaginable orogeny, the other allowing you to fantasise more proximate convulsions. Absolute time. Summer time. Conditioning and conditioned. Certainly you felt less guilty when you saw it that way. Merrier. Lighter. Though there had always been victims. The layers upon layers of fossils. Somebody eaten by his dogs because he had seen too much. Virgins sacrificed to have the ships sail. And this man killed when a 275-million-year-old rock pitched him down fifteen stories. How annoying the widow had to turn up now to take the shine off his revelling!

What he would like to do with Margaret was something ultimate, unique, something that went beyond all this slow accretion of similar exploits, stories that could be swapped in pubs and books, something that would be the sum of all his fantasies, and surpass them too. An epiphany. Whereas Thea he would merely have rogered. In the foreman's sound-proof cabin perhaps. While the gangsaws shrieked and slabbed. He shook his head. The local wine was strong. Nor was he used to the ferocious brightness bouncing off this quartz-white sand, the explosive colours of the sunshades, the long rows of enticing bodies. Usually when they sent him out on inspection, it was coarse aggregates in the Midlands, a look at the lithology of an armourstone for some breakwater: lunch in a pub, a small hotel. Write up the report on the train coming back.

Peter walked. The beach was split into so many bathing stations, each with its own distinctively-coloured sunshades anchored at regular intervals in the sand. This precarious strip of erosion and deposition was thus marshalled into the familiar human pattern of geometric squares following one hard upon the other: floor tiles, paddy fields, parquet, city blocks, high-rise façades, map grids, chessboards. Presumably they must be ready as ants to reimpose this order when the occasional storm washed all away. So money was at stake. Walking along between sunshades and seashore, he noticed that the normal detritus you would expect to find on a beach wasn't there. The driftwood, dead fish, and other unsightly victims of the land's edge had been cleared away, so as not to offend the bathers rushing in and out of the water, their polished flesh and lusty cries. He must check whether the hotel itemised its bills. Murray knew Anna, and in any event, the rent of a sunshade would be difficult to explain to Accounts.

The bathing stations had names, and numbers too for tourists unfamiliar with the language. Unless it was just a question of catering for those who would always see the similarity rather than the difference. He found station twenty-two and counted five rows back from the sea. But no, he would sneak up and tickle her. Or perhaps, if she had her eyes closed, he could wet a finger with saliva and slither it across the soft fat at the top inside of her legs. He went on to row six. The sunshades were concentric circles of fluorescent green and orange, each with its reference number, its deckchair, its lounge bed. Beneath them: a grandmother knitting, three adolescent girls chattering, mother and child, fat man with paper, infants digging . . .

Then he saw Mrs Owen's young daughter. Of all people. His heart sank. The girl was helping a toddler to fill a bucket. She looked up and recognised him. They didn't greet each other, but it was clear she had registered his concern, and understood. She, too, felt embarrassed by her mother. She, too, just wanted to live and have fun, not harp on their misfortune. He passed her and found shade fifteen, row six, fortunately vacant. In the row in front, barely ten feet away, Margaret was wearing a simple green and white two-piece. There were all the curves he wished to sate himself on, the skin he had never smelt in sunshine, the hair, the tall neck . . . and this Australian woman beside her on the deckchair: talking, talking, talking. It seemed so unnecessary. Such extraordinarily bad luck. In a place where every other blemish had been removed for those taking a holiday from their normal lives.

Unseen, he sat in the vacant deckchair in row six. He

had his back to them now: Margaret, who he had meticu-
lously planned to have to himself, and this Cassandra
figure fully dressed in black skirt and blouse, the only
dark spot on the whole beach, except for himself perhaps,
still in his business clothes.

Through the clamour, beneath the sunshades, he lis-
tened to their talk. The widow was describing her husband, how much she had loved him, how intense their
relationship had been. Now she was showing the photograph with the chipped tooth. What a fine, what a special
man he was! There was so much still to be lived and
settled between them. Their love had been so . . . Hearing her urgent voice, Peter remembered how Margaret,
just by being the way she was, had almost immediately
prompted the same kind of confession from himself,
though he had been describing a reality she made him
want to escape, rather than something he could never
return to. Going from tearful to angry, Mrs Owen said,
'And now they want to palm me off with some shame-
ful compensation, as if a person could just be paid for,
could be measured in money.' But she would get back at
them. She had a plan. It was the way they just sailed on
regardless that was so frustrating. 'They just don't seem
to understand that Jerry was Jerry.'

Jerry. So the victim had a name now. Peter looked up
and met the little girl's eye a few yards away. His own
daughter was younger though. Then she went back to
her play, lining up sand pies held together by the surface
tension between damp grains, the angle of repose near
vertical. The toddler she had adopted promptly trod on
them and giggled. Peter removed his jacket and arranged
it over his head as if to sleep.

'The truth is,' he heard now, 'people are just sacrificed
so the buildings can go up faster and the various interests
can start "realising their investment."'

Margaret's reply was so soft he couldn't pick up what

she said. He had told her almost at once that she had the voice of sea in a shell, a mermaid's whisper. It had utterly seduced him.

'You're here with the geologist?' the Australian woman said abruptly. 'Isn't he much older than you?' But at the same time a tannoy crackled to life and after a rumbustious jingle began to advertise local restaurants and entertainment in four languages. Apparently there was a bowling alley, a place where fish and chips could be bought, foreign beers, a McDonalds. Sameness was at a premium. Or as if an identical chequerboard picked up again after all the mountains and sea. There would be a beach barbecue, a lottery. Two minutes passed. Three. Four. As an afterthought, it was suggested one might visit a municipal museum, an archaeological site, the nearby island volcano. Came the jingle again, the details of a raffle. Then he realised Mrs Owen was on her feet, gathering her bags, looking for her daughter. But he was safe in the dark of his jacket.

'Wendy, Wendy! Come on!'

He waited, counted out a minute, then slipped round the deckchair and surprised her with his tongue on her navel. Margaret jack-knifed up from the lounge bed and laughed and laughed.

She had put his costume in her bag. Their two skins in the sand breathed together. His sense of well-being was extraordinary. With Margaret, equilibrium was not a question of having adapted to a rut, adjusted within to pressures without, but as if one had overflowed into oneself. In unlimited space, the heat welded them together. A shared moistness of touch. Complete unreality in this world of bright light and sharply-profiled colour. They chatted, Peter and Margaret, both so attuned that neither would comment on what to anybody who knew them must seem most obvious and most urgent. Rising through the transparency of the afternoon, their words were bubbles, with the buoyancy and inconsequence bubbles have. He whispered all he would do that evening and she chuckled. Until just the sheer wonder of it made him remember his dream.

———— • ————

The hotel reception desk was another long slab of the suspect local granite. Certainly it took a high polish, despite obvious discontinuities and alteration in the feldspars. Lifting down the suitcase the Australian woman had left for him, he had the shock of finding it far heavier than muscles and tendons had expected, so that he almost let go. Shoulder and elbow were wrenched tight. This was certainly not the specific gravity of the papers she had promised.

Then as they moved towards the lift, the receptionist called him back. A telephone call from London. And he thought it would be better to speak in the privacy of the booth in the lobby. It was thus that Margaret went ahead to their room and found the fax which had been slipped under the door.

Murray's voice from King's Cross was perfectly clear. What on earth was going on?

'In what sense?' Peter felt like a child caught in torchlight.

'This Dr Maifredi has been on the phone to the proprietors in Sydney. He was demanding to know if the construction people were trying to hold his company responsible for the death of this bloke.'

Peter relaxed.

'You mean Owen?'

'That's right.'

'Can he really be that stupid?'

Putting down the widow's suitcase, he wondered how

on earth she had managed to carry it around.

'He's not stupid at all. I suspect he was just using it as a ploy to get them to tell him why you *are* there. What worried me, or rather the Aussies, was that you might have let something slip.'

'Not at all.' Though he remembered how quick off the mark the quarry manager had been when he had told them only half the slab had fallen.

'Because this is a big deal in money terms.'

'I appreciate that.'

'If we can help the Australians out they'll be grateful.'

'I know.'

'You realise . . .'

'I said, I know.'

After a pause, Murray asked if he had come up with anything. Peter talked about a certain slap-happiness. They could play on the fact that the company was state-owned and workers didn't seem motivated. Poor observance of tolerances, poor inspection. What could you expect to find in just two days mooching about? They were certainly supplying at least two other big projects. Then the quarry plan was bad, the face too narrow to absorb the amount of explosive they were using. Murray felt this last point was interesting, because easily demonstrable. But none of it amounted to half what the other side could get on the Australians if they were at all smart about it.

There was a pause across a thousand and more miles.

'There are always the microfractures, right? Visible I hope.'

Peter said yes, but with the slabs only 25 millimetres thick they were inevitable.

'Look, I want you to stay on a couple of days. What we need is something really damning.'

This was unexpected.

'What if there isn't anything? I can't say there is if

there isn't.'

'If there isn't, there isn't,' Murray said. But it was clear there'd be a bonus if there was. For Peter, the postponement of a return to reality was bonus enough in itself.

'Except you'll have to tell Anna,' he told his senior partner. 'She hates me being away.'

'Will do,' Murray laughed. Murray always laughed when Peter mentioned his wife. It was irritating.

Day Three

The were two diverging slopes of drab London chert. The grass cover was sparse and the soil thin. He had bored deep and found all that was left of millennia of intense weathering. Once abundant groundwater had dissolved away all the limestone, leaving only a compaction of these hard, dark nodules of flint and chalcedony. What to do with it? Exploitation as a crushable aggregate should be feasible. A reasonable roadstone perhaps. Certainly the territory offered few other possibilities. Too bleak for crops or animal life. Too sad to leave as it was. Then, gathering his tools on the bare slope, tears in his eyes for what had been and what was, he became aware of a faint rumbling. The ground beneath his feet trembled, vibrated, as if an army of heavy trucks were passing. A million years were squeezed into an instant: the plates shifted, the magma rose, a huge intrusive body, forcing its way up. The surrounding rock was heated beyond the point of no return. The crystals lost their grip on each other. It was as if he saw deep deep inside the hill. He was the hill, and all the chained elements breaking free. Then, along the main fissure, huddled in a foetal ball and shooting upwards with a thousand melting boulders and the endless flux of planet earth's detritus, came the child. Same old chemicals in human form. And he saw the embryonic face. It was laughing for joy. When the whole hill exploded.

Sitting up, waiting for the dark to ease its fingers on his eyes, he reflected that he dreamt more when he slept with Margaret. He became more sensitive and volatile. There was a need to change. Every nerve was exposed. Whereas the cold temperatures of home suited his inner structure. He was in frozen equilibrium there. The elements couldn't hurt him. Through the muddle of his dispersing nightmare, Peter felt a faint itch of regret for that simple, henpecked homebody he had been.

Time was important in these nervous states. But the route to bed had hardly been of the most obvious and he couldn't find his watch. Finally, from a muddle of clothes on the floor, a reliable quartz crystal told him it was almost five o'clock.

There was a small lamp above the desk. He rummaged amongst dirty tissues in the wastebin and unsquabbled his wife's fax. 'Test positive. You to play.' The way she would never, never let him go. Ineptitude? Or vindictiveness? And he reflected that once again Margaret had excelled herself. First in her intuition, which he had immediately decided not to quarrel with. Then in her understanding. She truly was a pearl. And what surprised you most wasn't its beauty, but the smooth roundness of it, the serenity. Though there were times when the swine might have liked to have other piggies cast before them. Because this was simply breaking his heart. He squabbled up the fax again. Perhaps he was still in time to be the first man informed of fatherhood by fax. Unless it was imminent abortion. Anna would always double or bust.

A sleepy voice asked him what he was doing. He was going to look through the papers the Australian woman had given him. 'At this hour?' He couldn't sleep. He bent down and released the locks. Inside, the suitcase was divided in two. On the one side was a bundle of files; on the other, wrapped in clear polythene, a broken slab of polished stone. Even in this poor light he could see that the large, unnatural stain was blood. And caught on one jagged corner was a congealed scum of skin and hair.

———— • ————

Does one guilt cancel out another, or are the two added together? Or even multiplied? Can you separate them, saw, slab and polish, examine one by one, take a photomicrograph? Or do they just run together like slurry, forever torpid and amorphous? A family scheming to destroy itself. A mêlée of desperate soldiers. In a report entitled MARLBOROUGH PLACE PROJECT: THE FAÇADE, he read:

'POST TENDER AND PRIOR TO EXECUTION OF HEAD CONTRACT
(i) CCL did not accept responsibility for the design of granite fixings.
(ii) CCL did not accept responsibility for performance of granite supplier if that contract was assigned to them. Hence the provisional sum for supply of the granite was deleted from CCL's scope of works, in accordance with Head Contract Clause 3.10.01 (b).'

So much for the construction company. In the report presented by GRC, who were producing the prefab formwork that held the slabs, he read:

'Designs shown on drawings at tender time were top and bottom fixings with slabs resting on a thin ledge. The architect, Loper Aran & Partners, had a stated intention to use fixings supplied by Hans Putz of Germany. This type of fixing proved to be unsuitable in the particular application for this project, as it clashed with the joint seals for the panels. Also the geometry of the fixings did not suit some of the

29

gaps between stones, such as at corner columns.
Loper Aran then changed the design philosophy
to side fixings with pins inserted into holes drilled
in the vertical edges of the stone . . .'

And that stone was only 25 millimetres thick, already chosen on other criteria, already being cut and finished, with extensive microfractures, with phenocrysts more than a centimetre wide. Certainly it had been along the throat of the fixing hole that Jerry Owen's slab had failed.

'Well?' Margaret asked.

'The woman should get another husband,' he said.

'No, I mean, this stuff she's given you to read.'

'She must have got someone who had access to all these offices to copy it for her: the constructor, the prefab people, the architect, the proprietor. But I don't expect it's confidential. Maybe her husband had already got hold of some of it if he was worried about the project. He was somebody in the unions, I gather.'

'But does it help?'

'In what possible way?'

'Well . . .'

'You mean, in the sense of establishing whose fault it was?'

'Yes.'

'They all pass the buck, don't they?'

'But it must stop somewhere.'

'No, it goes round and round. Listen. This is a telex from the proprietor company to the supplier:

'"As you are aware, production of prefab units is underway in Brisbane. Difficulties are being experienced in relation to quality control of the material being supplied. We have attached an analysis, together with an overview for your information. Every effort must be made to overcome these problems, particularly in respect of the following:"'

He read quickly:

'"1. Of the 557 stones checked, 7% have failed as a result of being in excess of 27mm thick or less than 25mm thick.
2. Of the 557 stones checked, 3% have failed as a result of hairline cracking immediately adjacent to the fixing holes. It would appear that the fixing holes have been drilled too quickly, to the extent whereby heat is causing structural damage to the stone.
3. Of the 557 stones checked, 3.5% failed as a result of throat dimensions being less than 7mm."

'And so it goes on.' He threw the pages back on the desk.

'But that means the supplier is responsible.'

'Not at all. It means that somebody else is responsible for choosing the slabs before they are actually mounted. It also means the architect is criminally ignorant, since nobody could meet tolerances like that with this kind of granite.'

'And so?'

'I suppose you might find a legal expert to tell you who was technically responsible. Anyway, that's not what's at stake, frankly. I'm not here for that. There's already a verdict of accidental death.'

'So what shall I tell her if she comes to the beach again? I felt so sorry for her.'

'To relieve herself of the weight of this stone and get another husband.' Then, with that shift in his voice somebody like Margaret couldn't fail to recognise, Peter said, 'Don't you ever find yourself thinking that people are two a penny? You know, without putting too fine a point on it.'

There was a short silence in the hotel bedroom.

'You mean if it wasn't me it would be somebody else?' she asked.

She had her head cocked to one side. Her copper hair. Which would fade. The sheets drawn up over her slim, but not perfect, body. The rather thick calves were disappointing when she wore a skirt. Above all there was the face: unconventional, a faintly wry lopsidedness which was so much her personality. A shrewd tenderness. And the tall, pearly neck you just wanted to fall on and weep.

But he said, 'Yes, I suppose so.'

'Yes, for me too,' she said. 'Of course. There would be somebody else. But it wouldn't be the same, would it? Promise me,' she said, 'it wouldn't be the same.'

'It wouldn't.' He was shaking his head from side to side. 'It wouldn't, it wouldn't, it wouldn't. I promise. It will never be the same.'

He remembered having promised this before. Though he did mean it. And it was true. For all the intensity would then ripple out into other areas of life, other adventures perhaps, till the impulse exhausted itself, the elements stable again in some other arrangement.

'After we get back, we must stop seeing each other,' she said.

He took it in silence. She had already said she couldn't risk being responsible for what his wife was obviously threatening. Their relationship was wonderful, but she found it weighed on her too. It was a burden.

After a long pause, he said, 'Okay, but while you're here, you have to agree to do everything I want you to.'

'Okay.' She was bright. 'It's a deal.'

'Sodomy,' he elaborated, 'cunnilingus, mutual masturbation, fellatio . . .'

'If you can find some nicer names, please.'

'Not love?' he laughed.

They were gazing at each other. Gazing. There was her winsome face, bright eyes. And he knew she was happy to have had this easy chance to make her decision. Which was also an ultimatum. As he was not desperately unhappy thus to be presented with one. Now, perhaps, he would find out what his shear strength was. A little test. Almost laboratory conditions. Moving to kiss her, it appeared there was still everything to play for.

———— • ————

Again the bright light, the silent drive into eroding hills. Here and there, at a hairpin, across a slope, the intrusion that had formed the landscape outcropped in pale, monolithic chunks. Or where they had cut the hillside to widen the road for lorries there would be a fresher wall of it, lichens grabbing hold where the feldspars decayed to clay. A derelict hut had been built of rough blocks and topped with flaky slabs of schist.

Again he closed his eyes and turned them to the light. Such dazzling simplicity amidst all these complications, and yet the source of energy that fuelled them. It had been sunlight on their shoulders had prompted him and Anna to make love for the first time for a long time. She had told him she was safe. And now him to play what? The cards required were conventional gestures it should be easy to make. If they could reproduce serpentine in extruded plastic, what problems would the traditional trappings of reconciliation and commitment present? On behalf of a greater good. Especially if people really were so replaceable. The sunlight was simple through his eyelids at first, a field of garnet red, but then began to break up into waves, lines, sparkling patterns, not unlike some unimaginable photomicrograph taken over hundreds of millions of years as the minerals formed and separated. The cells. The phosphene.

Again Thea was at the plant gates. But today he did not think they had overestimated his importance. Rather the opposite. There was something Murray hadn't told him. Some deal. The Australians needed to nail their suppliers. At all costs. They wanted the most damning report imaginable delivered by a respectable specialist. Himself. Thea was here to distract his attention, to disarm him, to see that he didn't claim to have seen anything he hadn't. Perhaps to stop him seeing something he should. His principal responsibility was towards the company of which he was a partner, and then the client who was paying (handsomely) for his expertise. At the same time, he decided that if at all possible he would have sex with his guardian interpreter. He would be cheerful and relaxed and have a go. Because she was beautiful. Because the light excited him. Because she seemed the kind of person who would consider such an encounter casual. Because in this way he would begin to get over his mistress, whom he loved. He could substitute her even as she prepared, very wisely, to abandon him to wife and family. And dimly he sensed that in the willed emotional vertigo that must ensue, something might simply disintegrate. He had always half-admired those people who made their lives too complicated to suffer: three marriages, five children, mistresses. The pain of shear lay in the resistance surely, not the breakage. Or what if he were just to melt away into the light? Would that be the revelation? Certainly there was no need to think in terms of guilt and evil. But then, climbing out of the car, he saw another vehicle tucked into a small lay-by the other side of this winding road. And Mrs Owen was sitting in it, all in black again. Shaking Thea's hand, he sensed those eyes on his back.

Again, on entering the finishing plant, he felt ill. The noise, the stones. Everything was the same. The same grinding descent of the bladeframe, millimetre upon millimetre. The hours and minutes and days were being slabbed here along with the granite. The dark lines of the machines gave form to the workers' lives, as they gave form to the blocks. They set up territories and relationships. Twenty-four hours a day. Everywhere there were racks for semi-finished stones, boxes for waste and rubble. Men moved purposefully between them. Back and forth. Tracing patterns. Between this island and Australia too. Establishing a rapport, a new equilibrium. So that the screaming that pressed on his skull, even through the headset, was the scream of organisation, order, whereas the aspects of geology he had always enjoyed most were his crackhammer chipping away samples, his laboratory when he looked at what had come up from a grid of cores, a steel tip toying with the foliation of a blue-grey gneiss, those jobs where he said how things stood and left the rock where it was. Because once you actually started doing things to it, there was no telling what would happen. As with women. He grinned. Mother Earth. Pandora. His mind was full of patterning thoughts that never seemed to add up to anything.

Again he spent the morning measuring, calibrating, rejecting the most minute deviations. This wasn't difficult. Laying a straight edge across the surface, he found stones millimetrically out of flat. The wonder was that anyone could have imagined otherwise. For an hour and more he watched the men on the drilling jigs. He felt that this wasn't really his job. And the plant didn't seem very suitable either. Setting six bits in perfect linearity at such distances across three slabs, to then sink them with perfect perpendicularity into a material with a hardness rating of seven was clearly not what this particular machine had been designed for. Perhaps, three or four months ago, this very worker had drilled the hole whose throat had failed high in a blue sky. Unless the crane operator had indeed slammed the panel against the core structure. A moment's inattention. But this was not what Murray, himself and their clients must be concerned with. White overalls slipped over fashionable clothes, dust-mask protecting nose and mouth, Thea stood by his side. It was extraordinary how important sex had become for him these past few months. As if it held some key to his work too. Which was manifestly ridiculous.

Again he tried to talk to people. A man on a jig told the interpreter every how many working hours they checked and changed the bits. They were diamond-armed, water-cooled. Thea had diamonds in her ears, beneath the graphite hair. A watering mouth? He had remarked to Anna once how women often wore the hardest and softest of rocks together, diamond and talc. Diamond fingers masturbating thighs of talc. The glitter and the viscid give. Would Margaret? Yesterday evening . . .

'Mr Nicholson?' She had to shout right in his ear.

'Sorry?'

'No, it's just that you were smiling!'

Even when she shouted her voice had an unnatural, accentless quality to it, neither English nor foreign, but just the language being spoken.

'Nothing,' he shouted back.

'You looked very amused.'

The expression on her face might have been complicity. Or a pose for a photograph. And he rejected a stone for excessive hole diameter. The slab would vibrate in the wind. The soft, neoprene sheath would be worn away. The granite would rest on the bare steel pin, staining, fretting. Until in the next millennium a pedestrian looked up to see a stone tumbling from heaven. And it would not be a god.

Again they found their way to the foreman's sound-proof cabin. Again the man seemed resentful. Did he actually know how the façade slabs were being fixed? He had seen the original tender, yes. But when they had added the side drilling, had he considered why? His job, the foreman said, was to produce pieces of stone to the precise specifications given to him. He was a link in a long chain.

'Does producing work for three different projects at the same time mean you have to change the machine settings often?'

Thea presumably relayed the question he had asked. The foreman responded through her: 'We are giving priority to the Marlborough Place project.' Then speaking English himself, he added, 'Other specifications are for more thicker stone. Big tolerance. No trouble.'

Again Peter stood in the yard examining slab after slab. The sunshine was tall and brilliant on the polished surfaces. He was wasting his time. The enigmatic play of crystals told nothing. The microfractures were nothing more than microfractures. Perfectly acceptable. And the only way really to see if each slab was strong enough was to test how much shear it would take to break it. 'Lunch?' he asked. The quiet patience of this woman beside him had become a distinct pressure.

———— • ————

The nature of any silicate mineral is determined by the way in which the four oxygen ions choose to deploy themselves around each single ion of silicon. Beside the window of another small restaurant, Peter reflected that he had now eaten alone with four different women in four days: the lunch with his wife shortly before departure, an experience not unlike the pull-out test the Australians were using to determine the strength of those holes (ram in steel pin with sheath and heave out hard); the candlelit dinner with Margaret shortly after arrival, a long lava-hot fantasising of the thousands of little ways they would pleasure each other over the coming nights, with always the faint hope that something holy might be achieved, something revelatory; the embarrassing breakfast with Mrs Owen, who had recently lost what was most holy to her, a suitably frugal occasion; and now this business lunch with the too-beautiful interpreter who he would like to possess as one possesses an object of fashion, many objects, in a standard procedure, two particles just happening to come together in the same sedimentary bedding, without either the white heat of metamorphosis, or the slow rewards of lithification.

Four meals. So different, but all with women. As if the difference was simply a question of those people being arranged on different sides of himself in some theatrical tetrahedron. They held each other together, and him in tension. But Margaret had said it must end. It was a burden to her.

On his third glass of wine, he said, 'Tell me about yourself.'

Thea laughed. 'Why?'

'Because I'm having lunch with you. Because I'm intrigued.'

'Why intrigued?'

'It's rare to find a beautiful woman working in a stone company.'

'It's a beautiful product,' she objected without a hint of objection. Or modesty. 'A fashion product in its way. Why shouldn't a woman work there?'

'All the same, I'm intrigued.'

'And you want me to tell you about myself?'

'Yes.'

She was constantly smiling. 'By which you mean?'

'Where you come from, where you learnt English so well. Your family.'

She shook her head. The jet black hair was almost blue. 'Can't you see who someone is just by looking at them, Mr Nicholson? You don't need a life history, do you?'

He wasn't sure if this was a tease or a philosophy. Still, he felt so carelessly buoyant. That unreal buoyancy of a balloon cut free from its string. Or gas escaping from a borehole. He laughed. 'Then you will have to forgive me if I look at you quite closely.'

Which he duly did. But staring into his business contact's eyes, he saw nothing but the translucent perfection of the hazel iris. And in the black pupil, a reflection of himself looking. An enigma.

She laughed out loud at his pantomime of scrutiny. Their noses were only inches apart across the table. 'Well?'

He pulled a face. 'As before. You're a very beautiful woman. More I cannot say. Your family, birthplace, boyfriends, remain secret.'

She spluttered with amusement. 'You silly man!'

'Why?'

'Because you don't give a damn about my family and where I was born.'

Again they were looking at each other. It wasn't affection, but there was the pleasure of challenge.

'Do you?' she insisted.

He frowned. 'Okay, so what can you tell about me, just by looking?'

Her eyes narrowed over her wine glass. 'First, Mr Nicholson, that you are happy to be away from home, even when the job you are doing bores you.' She paused. Then smiled. 'And second, that perhaps you don't appreciate the danger.'

He felt as if pressure had suddenly been applied in a new and altogether unexpected direction.

'What danger?'

Unnecessarily, she wiped her lips on a napkin. 'It's just an impression you give,' she said. 'Like a little boy in a toyshop.' Her smile had a wink in it now.

'Nothing dangerous about toyshops,' he said. But then

from the corner of one eye, through the thinly-curtained glass beside him, he caught a glimpse of that same yellow Opel he had seen this morning parked outside the finishing plant. Again the shadow of a crane swept through the bright light across a fashionable building. Or as if someone had taken a surgical knife to his flirtatiousness.

'Have you met Mrs Owen?' he asked abruptly.

She didn't bat an eyelid.

'Why?'

'I just wondered how you could make your mind up about somebody like her without knowing her story.'

The interpreter had a fine patina of irony about her, which was her own special mix of beauty and intelligence; but something that rejected, rather than invited, penetration. The eye bounced off her.

She appeared to think. 'Well, you can see at first glance she's haunted. And that she'll never let go.'

'Yes, but unless you know what she's haunted by . . .'

'No,' Thea shook her head. 'No, because you can also see that if it wasn't that, it would be something else.'

In his mind a memory clicked: a case of linguistic isotopism, different words but in the same arrangement: You mean if it wasn't me it would be someone else. And this prompted him to make a different kind of substitution.

'But what if your husband got killed like that? How would you take it? Wouldn't you be doing what she's doing? Trying to find the guilty party. At least she has spirit.'

Thea leant forward, her smile faintly condescending. 'I would never have a husband, Mr Nicholson. Can't you see that?'

And of course he could. And Peter thought that when he had first seen Margaret, all he had known about her was that he wanted to know all. That was what her face told you. Your eye was drawn in. For a moment then he yearned to be starting out with Margaret, only Margaret, all the old fossils scorched away. It was a sudden violent tug at one corner of his heart. So that he was thoroughly perplexed by his waywardness. All the same he let himself be driven back to Thea's flat before the afternoon trip to Dr Maifredi's.

———— • ————

As if held together in solid solution, Peter Nicholson had been part of his wife, and she of him, for some millions of years it seemed. Then the temperature had fallen very slightly. Was that unimaginable in a semi-detached off Barnet Hill? The solution had begun to unmix, the crystals came apart. Could either of them be held responsible for such a process? Intellectually, this man had never put a finger on any particular moment or disposition. Yet responsibility and guilt were haunting concepts. Like plastics, they were never to be found in nature, but once invented you could hardly deny their usefulness. In any and every context. Peter knew that the night he dreamt there was evil in the rock, he had been dreaming about his marriage.

It had had nothing to do with Jerry Owen at all.

He had begun to study geology in his teens. He had been seduced. And ever since, he had loved to depersonalise, to find himself and all his actions in the material whose name he bore. So, the suburban nest of slow-growing crystals had come apart ex-solution. Leaving a couple of residual perthitic intergrowths: Sarah, Mark. The world could not be blamed for being in flux. Until, manipulating the time scale a little, Margaret had been the molten uplift from the core that had revolutionised his inner structure, rearranged all external faces. These were satisfying thoughts. He sensed there was strength in such parallels. They built up a lattice.

All the same, it was hard sometimes not to remember that one was a human being, apparently making decisions from one moment to the next, with a pregnant wife expecting a phone call, a mistress who had taken him to such white heat only to announce the imminent quenching, an unhinged woman following him around, screaming justice.

On a shelf in the interpreter's bedroom was a collection of desert roses: rounded petals of sand, smoothed, polished, cemented into complex symmetry by the Sahara wind. Laughing, she mentioned a holiday, a Land-Rover trek, a lover. She said she liked to think of life like that, wind-crafted, beautiful, detached. He did not remark how statistically rare it was, with all that volume of air racing across all that expanse of sand, for this phenomenon to occur. Though Thea was a very rare flowering herself. Quite perfect. And as he had somehow known, no emotion was required. Nor forthcoming.

Then they drove into the hills, but along the coast this time, a more wealthy area of stuccoed villas facing a bright southern sky, hazy sea. The intense light bred so much fine detail: the darkly etched cypresses marking the hairpins, the acid phosphorescence of the pines, the glassy – streaked leaves of the lemon trees. So that the eye from the moving car found itself seduced by a hallucinatory glow. Peter sat in a trance from which he did not wish to awake. As though life might be reborn if only consciousness were suppressed for long enough. But the man's house, when they arrived, was defended by tall railings, spiky iron gates, a dog.

Thea got out and spoke to a small video camera. The gates swung open. The drive was about a hundred metres of carefully sorted coarse aggregate, a limestone most probably, flanked by oleanders, flowerbeds. It was a rectangular world. On a square terrace above a blue lozenge of pool and below the trim pink wall of the villa, an Asian girl in crisp uniform appeared and offered drinks. He chose a gin and tonic which came in a square tumbler with prisms of ice, while the terrace, he saw, was paved with the company's granite: thirty-by-thirty centimetre tiles, perhaps only fifteen millimetres thick, but no structural stress of course. Just slippers and fashionable leather sandals to cope with. Thea had taken her shoes off. She loved, she said, how cool stone was in summer.

There was nothing rectangular about Dr Maifredi when he appeared. He was big, shambling, the fat spider in a delicate web. He wore loose shorts over chubbily freckled thighs. An open shirt. Thea stood up and he kissed the woman loudly on the mouth, squeezed her shoulder. She laughed, exactly as she had an hour before. A meaty hand shook Peter's vigorously and a little longer than necessary. The older man's head was bald, the eyes small and bright. But now he took dark glasses from a shirt pocket.

Thea announced she was going to take a swim. Her body swayed in skirts. He hadn't seen her bringing a costume.

Maifredi was watching him. 'Beautiful woman,' he said, with a strong accent. He chuckled. 'A great piece of girl.'

Peter said yes.

Maifredi continued to look at him. Each time he spoke it was with a grunting intake of breath. 'Maybe too beautiful, eh? What do you think?'

Peter smiled. There was an elegant travertine table between them where his drink refracted the light in faintly trembling curves on a cenozoic froth. Then the shadow of an awning began. Maifredi had taken care not to sit in the sunlight. Peter, who could never resist, felt its defining pressure on his shoulders. But didn't remove his office jacket.

Maifredi sprawled in a chair, scratched at a leg, grinned with a cigarette in his mouth. As though deliberately imposing a coarse vitality. He might fart at any moment. Coughing, he said, 'I was surprised you have come to see me, Mr Nicholson.'

'Why's that?'

'I imagined your instructions were no more than to inspect the finishing plant and quarry.'

'I felt it might be useful to talk to you about the whole thing.'

'Or perhaps you came for the girl.'

Peter allowed a slight smirk to cross his face. A little boy's smirk. In a toyshop? There was a splash. Automatically, he turned and saw her long body below, stretched supine in dark costume over the unnatural blue of a cement aggregate. An environment that suited her, a frame to her splendid physique. And she had been right to a certain extent about judging from appearances. Certainly one could tell from her smile on her back in the water that she would never reproach anyone for considering her an object.

Maifredi was silent, wriggling to scratch his back on his chair. They were looking at each other again.

'The nice thing about Thea is that she likes it, you know what I mean?' He was insistent. 'She likes the men.'

Peter said nothing this time.

'I think this is a good thing in a girl.'

'It can't be bad,' he agreed.

'But we are married men, Mr Nicholson.'

For the second time in as many days, it crossed Peter's mind as odd that someone should assume this so readily. Still, life was very pleasant on this terrace. The hot sun, bright light, cold gin. And at least the man was a character. Peter enjoyed a bit of men's talk. Which Murray always rejected. He could never run down his wife with

Murray. He said: 'Actually, there were two reasons why I came. First, I'd like to ask you if I could have the quarry manager at my disposal tomorrow morning. Second, I'd like to have access to your shear test rig.'

Maifredi smoked. 'A rather less attractive woman has come to visit me this morning, Mr Nicholson. A Mrs Owen.'

'Ah.'

'Actually I do not understand why she is here to shout at me, and not in Australia, to shout at Mr Lopez and Mr Aran.'

'I agree entirely.'

Maifredi called a name. The Asian maid reappeared and the fat man indicated Peter's glass.

'She is coming of course, because someone has made her to believe our company is responsible for her husband's death. She says she has read reports.'

'No, I think she's just a little unbalanced. It was a tragedy for her.'

Maifredi stubbed his cigarette out on the granite, which would not stain and could easily be cleaned. If not by the Asian maid returning with his drink, then by another.

'She says she has read reports. She does not come all the way from Australia for nothing.'

Peter said, 'I believe an inquest gave a verdict of accidental death. There was no question of anybody blaming anybody that I know of. It's certainly not part of my brief. These things happen when you tackle projects as big as Marlborough Place.'

'Especially, Mr Nicholson' – the fat man sat up – 'if you must tackle it in a such big hurry.' Then he slouched back as low as he could on his lounge chair. Constantly shifting, hugging himself, rubbing one knee against another, he seemed to revel in his physicality. From below came the sound of smooth, slow swimming, a machine-like regularity. The gin must have been at least a fifty–fifty solution.

'So, you know how much time they have lost when this man is killed?'

'Sorry?'

'You know how much time the contractors stop the work? How much delay?'

'I've no idea. That's not my department.'

'Then I tell you, Mr Nicholson. Two months.'

At least, Peter thought, he would be able to tell Murray it was as the Australians had suspected. The man was wise to it. 'And now,' the fat man added softly, 'they talk of redesigning the cladding.'

This the gin could not absorb into the warm glow of the afternoon.

'I beg your pardon?'

Still slouched low, Maifredi laughed. 'I see now I tell you something new.'

'What do you mean, redesigning the cladding?'

'They say to cut the slabs in half. We receive a telex this morning.'

'Just for the top storeys?'

'They have four storeys in stock. That is how I know they are hold up for two months while they wait to start again. The top twelve storeys will be so. Slabs cut in half.'

Peter said, 'Frankly, I think that's a wise decision.'

'It will reduce the insurance costs.'

'Yes.'

'And the unions are happier.'

'That too. Safer all round. To tell the truth I'm rather relieved.'

'But it will take much time, Mr Nicholson.'

'Yes, I suppose it will.'

'The frames prefabricated must be designed again.'

'You mean the formwork? Again, that's not my field, I'm afraid. What is it, glass-reinforced concrete?'

But Maifredi was not to be deflected.

'Do you know, Mr Nicholson, how much money they lose every month they have no rent for this project?'

'I've no idea.'

'You think: there are forty floors of space for the offices. Every floor is six thousand square metres. And there is the plaza for the shops. In the centre of Sydney.'

'A lot of money,' Peter accepted.

'About two millions of Australian dollars.' Maifredi belched and smiled. There was even a chuckle in his voice. 'So the reports our unfortunate lady has found are not about her husband's death. They are about time, Mr Nicholson. And your visit is about time also. About someone paying for lost time. About my company paying.'

There was a short silence. The fat man swirled ice in a glass, drank, swallowed loudly, scratched a shoulder.

'The stone is in the ground millions of years. But it must be dug out in months, minutes, Mr Nicholson. Somebody is in a hurry. As soon as you blast it from the hill, it is a race, a risk. Time and money, investment and rent.'

Peter said nothing. Then without thinking the thing through in any logical way, he decided to be entirely candid. It had to do with how he had been feeling lately. This extraordinary volatility. He could take no position and stick to it. His sensation was that of being constantly exhilarated and slightly sick. Unless it was just the gin.

He said, 'But surely, when they first came to you, Dr Maifredi, when you tendered for the job, you must have appreciated that these tolerances couldn't be met. With the kind of stone it is, the hardness, the size of the crystals, the pressure it was formed under, the geography of the deposit. You see, what I don't understand is how all this could have come about in the first place, how any company could have got into this position.'

Maifredi laughed. 'You are a nice man, Mr Nicholson, but you must understand that I know nothing about stone. Nothing at all. I cannot even tell you if it is marble or granite, or if you must cut it thick as the encyclopaedia, or thin as paper.' He laughed very loudly. 'You know what I study at the university? You know? I study classics. I am an expert on vase painting, Attic and Roman vase painting.'

'Yes, okay, but you must . . .'

'My job is a political appointment, Mr Nicholson. I am a member of a political party. I evaluate my work in political terms.'

'Yes, I'm aware that the company's state-run; all I meant to say was that you must have people advising you: engineers, technicians, who . . .'

What was disturbing was how completely confident the man seemed, how shamelessly he gathered and squeezed the flesh on top of his leg.

'You are meaning, someone must have told me this is an impossible contract?'

'Yes.'

'You are right, Mr Nicholson. They have told me with this thickness of stone and this affixing system there are problems.'

'Yet you accepted just the same?'

'They also told me this is a very big contract. One of the biggest.' He smiled. 'This is a political position that I have, Mr Nicholson. And jobs are a political question. By taking this contract, I have increased the persons that work here. I have assured votes to my party. I have got big money from the regional government for more investment.'

'And you have got a client who wants to sue you for a sum that would close the company down.'

'I have got an ignorant client that asked what is impossible. If I would not promise, another company would promise. Perhaps another company on this same island. A private company. He must sue his architect, not me.'

'He could perfectly well demonstrate that you knowingly made a promise you could not keep, that you were the experts in this field, not him, and that all things considered you could have got much closer to keeping that promise than you did, if only your organisation had been more efficient.'

There was a pause. During which Peter was able to reflect that Murray, who always played matters so close to the chest, would be furious.

Maifredi rubbed the fingers of both hands up and down heavy jowls. 'Presuming that the constructor is making his complain, the case must be at the International Chamber of Commerce, in London. Right? The arbitrator will know not much more about stone than me. Right? And in that case it seems the future of this company could very much depend on how convincing is your report, Mr Nicholson.' Smiling, he pursed his lips. 'Yes?' Then his eyes lifted. Thea was climbing the steps behind Peter's chair. Her radiant face and dripping body sparkled in the strong light.

'I was just reassuring Mr Nicholson,' Maifredi went on, 'that we do not expect his report is giving us particular problems. Certainly you must help him to see everything he wants to see.'

'Of course,' Thea smiled, with just half a wink to add an innuendo to this. 'Of course, whatever he wants.'

Then Peter was shown around the villa. There were open designer spaces, oriental rugs scattered over what must be white marble tiles inlaid with a central diamond of Azul Bahia blue. A dowdy woman was knitting by a window and Maifredi introduced his wife. Thea was in a red towel robe. And on shelves round the wall were scores of pots, jars, vases. Maifredi began to talk more simply and eagerly, a fat, gravelly voice, interrupted by wheezing and coughing. Here were the obsessive geometric shapes of the tenth century BC. Weren't they fine? Oh, copies of course. Though one wasn't. One was an original. Could his guest say which? Of course he couldn't, he wasn't an expert.

'If I broke them up and examined the clay, perhaps.'

'A rather drastic procedure only to establish a truth, Mr Nicholson.'

And here the geometry became more complex – they had got bored with such simplicity – intricate patterns that then gave way to the representative black-figure style of the great Attic period. Stark silhouetted figures on a bright white background. As if carved out of the light. The scenes were often violent: Apollo slaying Python, the knife at Iphigenia's throat, Poseidon's horses rising from the deep to abduct a nymph, Hades gloating over Kore. 'And this is my preferred one,' Maifredi said.

'My favourite,' Thea corrected. She smiled at Peter. The level of complicity was exactly as it had been at the factory gate the previous morning.

'Isn't it a beauty?'

On a large jar raised on a pedestal beside the staircase, a number of figures were in movement, one running as he carried another in his arms. 'This man is Theseus,' explained Maifredi. 'You can tell by his pony tail. He is abducting with this young girl. The two women that try to stop him are his wife Antiope and his mistress, the beautiful Helen. He sodomises her when she is thirteen years. And this is Pirithous, his friend, who is protecting his back. Wonderful times, don't you think, Mr Nicholson?' The fat man chuckled. 'Theseus was an obsessive abductor. The first man to imitate the gods in this.'

Out of politeness, Peter asked what the inscription beside the scene said.

Thea translated: 'I saw, let's run.'

———— • ————

On returning to his hotel this third full day of his trip, Peter Nicholson surprised himself by sitting down in the lobby. There was a small chandelier of the variety he had seen in several public spaces now. Its tassles of glass split the dull light into faint pinpricks of pink and blue. Other people sat in leather armchairs, on sofas. They pulled newspapers from a low table, again a glass surface with elegant enamelled legs. Then the floor, the walls, the ceiling, the stairs. Peter had the feeling he was stuck. Others were looking at their watches, waiting for contacts to appear, friends to meet. Certainly he had no lack of things to do himself. But as if a pattern that led you from one chequered square to the next had been removed, he felt lost, unable to find a way forward. All he could see were the endless details: a cloudy opal on an older woman's lapel, cigarette smoke drawn and then repelled by the revolving door.

Four months ago, in another hotel, the pattern that made each day a perfect mental copy of the one before had been undisputed. The checks and balances, the angles between the lattice of relationships, mental attitudes, financial commitments and capacities, had been in perfect symmetry. He was at home on his metalled ways, to the point that the slow cooling and just-perceived deceleration had become part of those ways, not so much acceptable as the only thing imaginable. Passion was a thing of the past. Sublimated in the essential geometry, frustration went unnoticed. In his hands, in that other hotel, he had held a brief relative to the shifting of a watercourse as a result of extensive quarrying in a sand horizon overlying impermeable clay. His client was being sued by a group of farmers. And the computer-typed pages, following one after another, entered his life with the satisfying obviousness of another meal, another shower, the wink of the cursor along the liquid crystal lines of his portable processor. He enjoyed it. He enjoyed the naturalness with which his analysis formed as all the elements fell into their allotted place: experience, theory, facts. Nor would he have dreamt of submitting a report that was anything but the truth as he saw it: the deceptively undulating contour lines of aquitard and aquiperm, the client's failure to investigate geological conditions immediately downstream of the quarry, the possible solutions. These things passed through him as metered water entering a pump and being dispatched along the constantly ramifying human gridwork, angle after angle. Not life slipping through his fingers, so much as a steady pulse beating the same even, machine rhythm. Margaret was the quarry foreman's daughter and shared his compartment on the return trip to London.

Within days he was smirking, complaining, restless, ecstatic, tense, confident, indescribably happy, desperate, scheming. The days speeded up and became interminable. He flirted with the secretaries, slept with his wife that one sunny day, and almost with a woman in the accounts department of a client in Halifax. But he had arranged to spend that night with Margaret in Birmingham and other encounters were only the delicious undertows that kept his wave of feeling for her in cresting tension. Work became an obstacle, a stone to be rolled uphill rather than patiently analysed. Yet he had moved heaven and earth to arrange everybody's schedule so that only he would be free for this Mediterranean trip. Indeed he had reached the point where he couldn't and wouldn't see beyond it: this holiday, these nights with Margaret, a decision perhaps, or a revelation. Then the delirium at the airport, the arrival, the love-making, Mrs Owen, Thea, the portentous fax, Margaret's sad announcement, the stone,

Murray, the ambiguous Maifredi. It had inspired a sort of vertigo. A sudden cobwebbing of cracks shivering through his personality. He couldn't move. As though what was left of life's old pattern simply ended here. In a hotel lobby, that should have been all too familiar. The back and forth of cigarette smoke by the door. The arrival and departure of people with despatch cases and newspapers. The even trilling of the telephone on the granite desktop and the unerring monotone formula of the receptionist's response. He felt quite lost.

A shadow passed right behind his chair. Came a high-pitched little cry, a hissed, Australian, 'Wendy, please!' No more than a yard away. Immediately he was released from his bafflement, jerked into action. When the lift door across the lobby was just about to close, he stood up and walked briskly over. The metal slid shut behind him. 'I saw,' he remembered, 'let's run.'

In his room he found Margaret's note on the desk. 'AT THE SUNSHADE.' And there was another fax in an unsealed envelope. His wife sent faxes because she liked to imagine the embarrassment they caused, seen as they must be by the receptionist and room service. She created drama. She lived in drama. For of course she would see it as a defeat for her to phone him rather than vice versa. This one said, 'Peter, why haven't you phoned? Please! I'm nearly three months. Even Murray has been more understanding.' He crumpled the paper up, tossed it in the bin and changed rapidly into the beachwear Margaret had left on the bed.

There came a knock on the door. After a silence it was repeated. Then the voice, the strong accent, its plangent individuality. 'I'd like to talk to you, please, Mr Nicholson.'

He pulled trousers over his trunks and said to come in.

Apparently she was very calm and practical, with that

sensible concentration of busy mothers in supermarkets.

'Hello, Mrs Owen.'

She walked forward into the room. 'You have been trying to avoid me.'

'Not at all.'

'Yes you have.'

'No, really. I've seen you on a number of occasions today, but none of them seemed the right moment to talk.'

'It's not important,' she said. 'The fact is I'm going back home the day after tomorrow, and I want to settle this before I leave.'

'Settle what exactly?'

'Who is responsible for my husband's death.'

He sighed. 'What exactly do you plan to do when and if you establish that?'

She made a gesture of impatience. 'That's my problem.'

He said there were cold drinks in the fridge near the bed. Would she like to sit down? Have something. 'I've looked through the papers you gave me,' he explained.

She sat on the straight-backed chair by the desk. There was something irretrievably plain about her square-jawed expression, loose dress, short, unwashed hair. But at least she was businesslike.

'And?'

'It's a mess,' he said.

'But I was right in coming here. It does point clearly to their responsibility.'

Feeling for an approach that would not be patronising, he said, 'Those reports you read were probably compiled with an eye to claiming a large sum of money from the stone supplier in compensation for delays to the completion of the building, delays brought about mostly by bad cladding design and the reluctance of the unions to handle materials they were suspicious of.'

'Because they were fractured, for God's sake! Jerry

knew that himself. There are photographs galore. Because these people are using too much explosive.'

He explained that she should be careful when giving credence to what she read and heard. 'Listen, if the construction company had been used to working with granite, they would have appreciated that microfractures are perfectly common. They open due to stress relief in the first month or two after cutting and then stabilise, assuming they are not subjected to too much shear. Since the fractures in question are not aligned and generally terminate at the boundaries of the quartz grains, they don't really present a serious problem, if properly handled. There's no reason why a slab should fail because of these microfractures. Given a decent fixing method.'

She was staring at him.

'Quality stone cladding has become a craze, Mrs Owen. Everybody's doing it. Everybody wants Greek and Italian marbles and granites sparkling on the fortieth and fiftieth floors of their office blocks. In Los Angeles, Tokyo, wherever. This same company is presently supplying a sizeable project in Seattle with no problems at all. It's just that unfortunately not everybody has had time to learn how to use the stuff.'

She said, 'My husband is dead. I want to know why.'

There was a moment's silence before he remarked, 'Perhaps this is more your own personal problem than a question for a geologist or construction engineer, Mrs Owen.'

Quite unexpectedly she burst into tears. She bent forward on the chair and shook and sobbed soundlessly. Peter went to a shelf above the fridge. There were bottles whose curious contents he was not familiar with. Then what seemed to be a brandy. He poured two dusty glasses and put one beside her. As he sipped he had the fleeting mental image of Thea's body, as it were superimposed over Margaret's, where she lay on the beach under a now slanting sun amongst the lengthening shadows of the green and orange sunshades. But he felt perfectly in control again.

'I'm sorry,' he said. 'I was unkind.'

She pulled herself together, found a tissue. The motions and gestures were so familiar. As when she had burrowed in her handbag for the photograph, or again the shopping woman's stubbornness when she had walked in a moment before. It was not so much that she reminded him of his wife, as that he constantly found himself confronted with these short circuits, these superimpositions. How unique could people be when there were so many of them? And he saw a way of assuaging guilt.

He sat down, drank and asked softly, 'The chip on your husband's tooth. How did he come by it?'

'I'm sorry?'

'Your husband. Jerry. He had a chip on a front tooth. I wondered how he had come by it? I'm sorry, it's a ridiculous thing to ask.'

'No,' she laughed, seeming to find relief. 'Can you believe I did it? We were playing racketball. You know. I was angry because I was losing. I made a wild swipe. Not intentionally or anything. I caught him on the mouth.'

Peter said, 'I got mine when somebody banged my head down on a slide at ten years old.'

She smiled. 'I hadn't noticed.'

Like most people, Mrs Owen was more attractive when she smiled. The standard, modern hotel room was sweetened with an unexpected intimacy.

'My wife,' he said, 'notices everything about teeth. It drives me crazy. You have someone to dinner and she says, "Two crowns and a bridge at his age! He'll be falling to pieces in no time." '

She laughed, but her voice was still nasal with tears. 'Jerry always noticed eyes. He said you had to have perfect eyes to be a fitter. You had to be able to read an angle like a book.' Then she said, 'But the woman you're with here isn't your wife, Mr Nicholson.'

'No.' Having wanted only to be rid of her up to the moment when she burst out crying, he now found himself suggesting she might as well call him Peter.

'And I'm Hazel.'

He laughed. 'Pleased to meet you, Hazel.' Then thought perhaps this good humour was just the wine over lunch, the champagne Thea had had in her fridge, Maifredi's two very serious gins, and now this glass of brandy.

'So?' she said.

'So what? I'm here with Margaret, that's all.'

Her eyes gleamed. 'It just occurs to me that a man betraying his wife can't really appreciate how I feel about Jerry. How angry I am. When they offer me compensation. When they say I should find another husband while I'm still young enough. For the sake of my daughter. Because at the moment I feel that this . . . this . . . search for whoever killed him, whoever was responsible for his dying, I feel it's the only thing that keeps me hanging on to life. Because I can't ever imagine replacing Jerry. He was irreplaceable. And when I see a man happily cheating on his wife because he's off on his business trip, I just don't see how he could even begin to understand. And obviously he won't make much effort to help.'

Peter could say nothing to this. Though of course he knew what he thought. You couldn't weep over every fossil. Only those close to you were special. To the rest of the matrix you could be entirely indifferent. Even behave with indifference. You did your job and that was that. Otherwise you'd be shelling out to every beggar on the street, mailing every salary to Oxfam. Jerry Owen was only one.

He said, 'I'm actually very much in love with

Margaret. Perhaps that helps me to understand.'

'Yet you spend the morning flirting with this woman who takes you around. Or so it seems to me.'

Peter opened his mouth, then sighed. 'Margaret will be leaving me when we go back.'

'So she told me.'

'If you know everything already, there hardly seems any point in talking about it.'

'I just can't understand why you two don't stay together if you are as much in love as she says.'

He felt his voice growing colder. 'Because as she probably also told you, I have two children and a wife who is apparently expecting a third. Margaret is not stupid. And neither am I.'

'But what about your wife? If you left her it would give her a chance to find somebody else.'

'She doesn't want to find anybody else.'

'She would if she knew what you were up to here.' The Australian woman added, 'I always think it's best when situations are clear and everybody knows where everybody is. The fact is . . .'

'Mrs Owen, if you don't think I can understand your position, please don't pretend to understand mine.'

'Hazel,' she said lightly.

'Hazel,' he accepted. But if he hadn't been unpleasant like that, something would have given.

There was a brief silence. Then she said, 'It's just sad. For you too.'

He tried to make that the end of it, smiling falsely, 'So what's new?'

'But I think if you are, if you are . . .'

'What?' he almost snapped.

'You see, I believe love can move mountains. If you . . . were to . . .'

'I don't believe so. Mountains generally only move as a result of isostatic adjustments over some millions of years.'

'But how can you be so cold?'

He shrugged his shoulders. 'I know about how mountains move.'

She was trying to do something to him with her eyes, staring. A quite tangible pressure. She said, 'Anyway, I told her to cling to you like hell, if she loves you.'

Peter ran his hand through his hair, then shook his head. This was too much. 'As you are clinging to your husband, perhaps,' he said.

There was a long silence, so long that he began to hear her breathing. Then she said, 'What I came here to say was, I'm leaving the day after tomorrow. So can I have my papers and things back, please?'

He said of course. 'I'd just like to keep the slab for a while, if that's okay. Until tomorrow at least.'

She was on to it at once.

'So, there is something?'

He shrugged his shoulders.

'Is there?'

They looked at one another, he still sitting on the edge of the bed, empty brandy glass in his hand. There was something unsettling about her flush of excitement. To what end?

'Look,' he said, 'are you quite sure that's the stone that killed your husband?'

'Of course.'

'How do you know?'

'I was there half an hour after it happened. It was still lying there on the scaffolding. There's the blood. I took it as a memento.'

'Yes, but didn't they want it for the inquest?'

'They said there was no need. What is it?' she demanded.

'There's something odd about it, that's all.'

'Which is?'

'Well,' he hesitated, 'it didn't come from the quarry I looked at here. And it isn't the same stone as the blocks they're cutting in the finishing plant.'

———— • ————

She started laughing even before his slanting shadow fell across her. Like a child who knows she's going to be tickled. He did feel guilt, but then immediately on moving into her presence, a yearning too. Something he was conscious of as never before. As though entering the magnetic field of his very own lodestone. If he could be here forever, all would be well. Or even, perhaps, if he had never found her. The guilt, and the excitement, lay in moving in and out of that field.

At seven o'clock the beach was emptying. Bathers heading home kicked up the coarse sand. Men were out on small tractors, sieving for debris and litter. This constant cosmetic effort. The lovers kissed and embraced, then walked down to the water.

'Have you phoned Anna?' she asked quickly. It was something to be got out of the way: a foreign body, a weight she needed off her mind. So he said he had, and that he had reassured her. 'But then I got held up by Mrs Antipodes.'

Margaret laughed. 'I feel so sorry for her. She spent all afternoon lecturing me about my having an affair with you. She's lonely.'

They reached the water's edge.

'She told me she'd told you to cling on like hell.'

'Yes, she did.'

'And you?'

Margaret's costume brought out the beauty of waist, bust and neck, but betrayed the slight thickness of thighs and ankles, a trace of varicosity. Tied up, her hair was polished copper.

'She sees everything in terms of her husband. I tried to be nice to her.'

Again his feelings rose so powerfully. Rigid structures of thought broke down in the head. So that he turned and embraced her, overwhelmed by a desire to go beyond desire. Their mouths closed.

'What was that for?' she asked.

'You're so wise,' he told her.

'I'll give you the examining commission's address,' she laughed. For she, too, was between lives, waiting for results. Everything depended on results of one kind or another. Then life would move on. She wanted to work abroad, see Europe, America. This love was a burden to her. She had said so twice, albeit with melting eyes.

They walked into water that was tepid and quite still. Above the horizon rose a volcanic island he still hoped they might have time to visit. She splashed him and launched into a swim. He followed, accepting the shock of immersion, until they were both treading water perhaps a hundred metres from the shoreline. Looking back, there was the rugged profile of the hills above the bay, all the fine detail of its vegetation, wild and cultivated, tones and patterns, and then the villas, the churches, hints of discontinuity where a road was, a telephone wire, a railway, interminable variation – all suddenly vanishing to stark silhouette as the sun dropped behind and glowed above the jagged edges. As if cut out of the light, he remembered.

And told her, 'You know you've got a tan.'

'I should hope so.'

'You're a sort of brown jasper.'

'Nice of you to notice.'

'Polished of course.'

'Of course.'

'Even marketable.'

'Not on your life.' She shook her head. 'How could

anyone possibly pay?'

'In kind, perhaps?'

Treading water, they exchanged a salty kiss. Then she began to swim and ducked below the surface, disappeared. Turning away from the sharply etched vision of the land, he found the sea by contrast entirely undifferentiated, uniform, faintly luminous in what all at once was dusk now. The surface was monotonously still across a vast expanse, flat, but for the roundness of the planet, a great leveller of sand and stones. The land and the sea; in a simple turning of the head. The one original amongst many copies on Maifredi's shelves. Jerry Owen in his photograph – alive and dead. How these opposites called to each other. There would be no faithfulness without betrayal.

She came splashing to the surface and tossed copper hair behind her, shattering the horizon in a shower of fine droplets. And they kissed again. Clumsily, for they had to kick to stay afloat.

'A small deposit,' he whispered.

'Deposit as in pre-payment, or tiny sediment?'

But he wanted to get beyond this little game and say something that might be important. Except that his feelings tended to inarticulacy. What might there be to say? A confession? A promise? To do what? To tear free from the rock, the binding lattice of home and children. He saw he had betrayed Margaret above all to ruin something so beautiful it was perilous.

She laughed and swam away again. She was the better swimmer. Again she ducked underwater. Alone in the evening sea, he heard the throbbing of the tractors cleaning the beach, the cry of youths kicking a ball, then a sharper drone, faint but swelling. He rolled over and scanned the horizon. But could see nothing. Still the drone grew louder. Until a dark speck detached itself from the mass of the distant volcano and was racing for the shore. A powerboat. Margaret bobbed up twenty yards further out. They formed a line: the racing boat, the girl, himself. He called to her as she looked about in a moment of disorientation. But the drone had become a roar. It was approaching so fast. As if from nothingness: Poseidon's horses storming up from the monotonous surface. For the rape. Margaret saw it and dived. Peter was as if frozen. The raised bow and a great mass of churned white twilit water raced straight at him. He panicked, floundering. The boat passed feet away. A boy and girl were arm in arm, laughing into the spray.

Later, in the hotel restaurant, they laughed themselves at what people would have thought, had the worst come about. The idea of being discovered after some accidental death was curiously gratifying. It would help, Peter said, to reconcile one's wife to the loss. You dropped something and it broke, but then you saw it had been rotten inside anyway. You thought, 'Oh well.' He chuckled. 'Think if Mrs Antipodes had discovered her bloke was having a homosexual affair with one of his fitters. What a release! She'd take the insurance money and run.' They laughed hard. Though knowing that the real reason for relishing this imagined discovery lay elsewhere. It had to do with being known, and vindicated and set free. Detached from the complexities of life, Anna would know him for what he was. The slab smashed and all the little particles in the aggregate were liberated from its constricting embrace. Or as when a family breaks up and everybody can breathe and regret. Peter ate fast and ordered more than he usually would. When the ice-cream came he asked her to slither a finger between her legs and then into his mouth. 'In a hurry to try everything at least once,' he explained.

Day Four

Tonight the censors were at work. He remembered nothing. But they were unable to persuade him there was nothing to remember. He woke with the sensation of being coughed up from utter darkness, the fragment of some vast explosion. Applying pressure, he tried to feel his way back down to where he had been. But he was pressing against a darkened mirror. There was nothing but his own groping.

Careful not to disturb, he got up and for the third morning running stood in the hotel room, saw the dawn on terracotta tiles, looked down at the porphyry fans in the street where a street-cleaning van inched along with droning brushes. There had been a machine in his dream perhaps. The sound of a machine. It was speculation.

He sat at the rickety hotel desk and again considered the report he was being paid to make. On opening the Epsom he found Margaret had left a message on the screen: 'Don't be afraid for me or of me, I love you.' His eyes narrowed and he inserted a disk. Then continued where he had left off:

'The company is a limited liability operation with government share participation. Basically, it is owned and run by the regional authorities. The effect of this is that, on the whole, the workers have an attitude not in accordance with the care needed for the production of finished work of the high quality required. During the visit, an attitude of carelessness on the part of the workers during the various stages of manufacturing has been evidenced. This is to be expected as the terms of employment of the employees, and also of their dismissal and/or sanction, are governed by political considerations. This is a severe problem for the middle management of the company who have little effective control. The following specific problems were noted:

1. The tolerances of the various dimensions of the finished products seemed excessive for the workers employed in cutting and polishing the slabs. Instead of adapting themselves to work to the tolerances, they appeared to refuse them.
2. Having seen some slabs during and after processing, it can be said that the quality and degree of polishing of the slabs seemed poor. Probably the cause was the use of unsuitable abrasives (too coarse, trading off quality for speed), and also an incorrect approach to the work.
3. The checking of the slabs for cracking was superficial. Slabs with evident cracking were accepted as perfect by some operatives; only after my intervention were the flaws recognised by them.
4. Some slabs, which had been accepted as perfect for thickness, were rejected only after my intervention because they were markedly out of permitted tolerances.
5. The holes for fixing, etc., in some slabs were so far out of their correct position that the inaccuracy was immediately visible to the naked eye, even before gauge and rule checks.
6. The machinery for fixing hole and slot drilling has design errors. It is this observer's impression that with the present machinery settings it would be more or less impossible to achieve compliance with the tolerances required.
7. Dealing with problems associated with hole drilling, it is important to mention, considering the

diameter of the holes and the presence of micro-cracking between quartz and feldspar crystals, that each hole drilled in a position where these mineral crystals are particularly profuse will likely result in damage to the slab.'

Closing the Epsom, he reflected that he was paid to tell half the story. It was in the nature of this game of exchanges that you played a part and somebody else deduced a whole. Certainly it wouldn't be these vague comments that would decide the court case. But beside him, leaning against the desk, was the broken slab the Australian woman had brought. He removed it from its plastic bag, careful to avoid touching the stains and that crusty patch of skin and hair. Running a finger along the jagged edge, a small, brown flake of biotite came away and tinkled to the floor. The colour of the stone must be all but identical, but on close inspection, the way it was achieved was quite different. The feldspar crystals were noticeably smaller, reducing the porphyritic look of the rock he had seen quarried at Palinu, and there was a more regular orientation, elongated flakes lining up across the slab, suggesting that this rock had come from the very edge of its pluton. He found his magnifying glass and moved it across the stone. Adjacent to the grains of biotite there were definite traces of weathering.

Outside, the sun must have topped the horizon, or a roof. Details sharpened quite dazzlingly and a slanting shaft boiled dust above the sill. He carried the slab over there and let the light explode on its polished grey surface. Beneath his lens all kinds of colours danced to the tune. Yellow grains and green, a trace of hornblendite perhaps, a tiny mauve tourmaline. Thousands upon thousands upon thousands of particles. And the hills were nothing else.

Shaking his head, he stood up, checked that Margaret

was still sleeping, walked downstairs and asked the receptionist to give him a line in the booth in the corridor.

'There is an envelope for you,' the girl said. He picked it up, saw the name of the company, then went into the booth and dialled. Waiting for the connection, looking at the floor, he wondered if people were never disturbed to find everything being mimicked and manipulated: here a compact, reddish limestone complete with styolites in frankly second-rate ceramics.

The electric pitter patter found its way through the maze of streets. The tones began. He drummed his fingers on the envelope, felt the size and shape of what was inside, then, with a sudden inkling, trapped the receiver between chin and collar and tore it open. 'Hello?' His wife's voice had the vulnerability of someone dragged from sleep. He had forgotten there was an hour's time difference as well. 'Hello, who is it?' Frozen, he held the receiver still. 'Who is that please?' He pressed a finger on the cradle. In his other hand was a thin wad of banknotes.

———— • ————

Sedimentary rocks cover two-thirds of the earth's surface, but account for only a tiny fraction of its weight and volume. The debris goes back and forth, the clasts, the decayed organic matter, the chemicals dissolved and precipitated. Bedding planes are compressed, lithified, buckled into hill or valley, beautiful or barren, until the slow drift of the continents finally drags them to some plate boundary beneath the sea to be sucked back down into basalt and mantle, melted, rendered formless, beyond the reach of all examination, all remorse. And the sun, Peter thought, in the car they sent for him again, was another all-conditioning factor you could never look at. Only cut things out of. The everyday, sedimentary life.

But granite was not a sedimentary rock. It rose straight

from the centre: an intrusion of extraordinary heat and intensity, forcing its way up through the crust, metamorphosing all around it. Still, the surface always won in the end, converted all to itself. The intrusion cooled and decayed, the weathered rock yielded its minerals to the soil, became plants, a tree, a child, or was quarried to make the walls of the child's bedroom, or a butcher's slab. Peter had the fatal stone in his suitcase as he watched out of the window at the same sun, the same hills, noticing today a primitive broch-like tower, stark on the slope above. More than a thousand years BC, the airline brochure had explained of this characteristic feature. Barely an atom of geological time.

Thea was waiting in her car. She stood up in jeans, a neat jacket, modelling all that was on and around her. He had never had sex with such a beautiful woman. Never had sex so lightly, so capriciously. Yet it was as if he hadn't penetrated her at all. There was nothing that drew them together here this morning but their jobs. In two or three days he would be back with the wife he hadn't phoned after her announcement of pregnancy had ruined (perhaps deliberately) his carefully planned trip. As if she knew. And though the same suspicion could hardly be levelled against Hazel Owen, the effect of dead husband, chipped tooth and cries for justice, had been much the same. Why had he slept with Thea? Certainly there was precious little light coming through this crack in his personality. Peter reflected that of all this eagerly awaited trip, only day one, only day one had been without a shadow. And now was almost forgotten.

The quarry had been extended deep into the hill, forming a small artificial valley. Presumably they were pushing it deeper, rather than expanding the face, because of the time it would take to clear the slope to one side and perhaps open a new access track. The Marlborough Place contract was no less demanding in terms of volume per month than in terms of tolerances. Then they were supplying others, too. They had clients they didn't wish to lose. This was understandable. Still, the end result was that when the workers retreated and the penthrite and Tutagex ignited beneath columns of water, there was nowhere for the shock waves to escape except through the hard crystal matrix that was the quarry's asset. Presumably the management were perfectly aware of this.

He asked if he could put his bag down. Thea pushed the door of a low prefab set up in the space roughly cleared for parking. There was a desk with computer, a chair, a drinks machine, and beside each dust-obscured window the men had pinned pornography. Pirelli. The mass production of polished perfect women. The slabbing of intimacy. He left the bag on the desk.

Picking up green overalls from a heap by the door, Thea asked, 'Do you like the pictures?' But even now it wasn't quite a reference to what they had done yesterday. And it was curious how this coolness of hers was simultaneously disturbing and reassuring. In almost a perfect reverse image of the way his passion for Margaret had been, was, reassuring and disturbing.

He asked, 'Do you?'

'I think everybody likes pornography,' she laughed. She was wriggling into the overalls.

'So there was no need to ask.'

'But not everybody says they like it.'

'So perhaps "like" is the wrong word,' he said. 'Maybe fascinate would be more accurate.' He was aware of an element of challenge, even defiance, when they spoke. As though something were at stake. They must beat each other. It was making him think very fast. 'And people don't always like to be fascinated. They find it coercive. So they say they don't like it.'

He looked straight at her. But her smile, doing up

a button, was as inscrutable as those on the photos round the wall. A man smothered in dust from top to toe came in and pushed the buttons on the dispenser. There was the inevitable machine hum. Ignoring it, she asked in a casual voice, 'So, do you like me, or are you fascinated?'

'I think you'd prefer for me to be fascinated.'

She laughed. Everything was a source of amusement. 'You see,' she said, 'how much you can learn about people without knowing where they come from or whether their grandparents were farmers or gangsters.'

Peter said, 'I must say, though, that I never actually buy pornography, fascinated as I am.'

This really made her laugh. There were her bright eyes and teeth, the saccharoidal quality of white skin set off by graphite hair, which she was now twisting into a bun to put her safety helmet on. She drew a breath to say, 'I hope you didn't think I'd be offended by that.' Despite the worker taking his coffee, she leaned forward and kissed him on the lips.

And yes, Peter was fascinated by her. As though by a danger that is too exciting. The way he felt drawn to those great bladeframes grinding back and forth. A death wish of pure sex. In a monotone he said, 'I'd like to make love to you with your helmet on, from behind.' She smiled, blandly. So that he wondered if he had split in two yet, or three, or if the cracks were still reasonably tight and stable and he would, after all, remain securely suspended on the respectable façade of family and domesticity for ever and ever.

It was nine thirty. The sun was already high and hot. The crude geometry of the quarry was thus given an added dimension of brilliant light and deep shadow. Cut into the dull green of the hillside, the whitish banks of rock stood out starkly like giant steps. To where? A big front loader with caterpillar tracks was shoving a block of some tens of tons across the quarry floor to where a derrick was mounted for sorting the stone and lifting it on to the trucks. The engine roared and strained as the enormous weight ground across the surface. Chips and sparks flew. Until the rock jammed against a small acclivity. The driver backed off, then attacked again. The engine screamed. Instead of shifting the block, the back of the tracks came up. The big yellow loader wobbled like a toy. The din in the three enclosed walls of the quarry was infernal. Abruptly, the stone shifted and the tracks came down with a crash.

He asked her if there were ever any accidents.

One death, she said, and two serious injuries. Over three years. An average price to pay for these quarries.

They found the manager above the face and climbed twenty feet up a steel ladder. He was supervising the delineation of a new area to drill and blast out. The weathered overburden had been removed for about twenty metres beyond the face. The problem was a thin dike, perhaps ten centimetres wide, cutting obliquely across the intrusion from the right-hand corner of the face. A glance at the scraped surface suggested some kind of mineralisation from the granite mass itself, darker, rich in iron. This would inevitably reduce the volume of the next few days' output.

Peter watched as the men measured and smoked, arguing in their own language. There were some heated exchanges, as if something was somebody's fault. He recognised a told-you-so whine in one man's voice, as one might recognise a shape without appreciating material or colour. The sun was a physical pressure on everything, an intensification of gravity, honing every line for better grip. Was Margaret on the beach already? Tanning. What nights they had had! What explorations! What quarrying of joy and sadness! Finally, the youngest man took a spray can and began to mark out the lines. On this advance they had decided to lose a wedge-shaped triangle accounting for perhaps thirty per cent of the face. Assuming they didn't change the direction of excavation, they would have to lose similar volumes on the next two advances, before recovering the entire face as the dike ran out. A small group of men began to set up the drill steels. The quarry manager came over to them.

'Annoying,' Peter said.

Thea dutifully translated, but the quarry manager preferred to show off his English. Small, squat, friendly, but with sharp features, he might have been one of any number of shrewd, practical men Peter came across on his travels. Except that in England perhaps they didn't wear dark glasses.

'There are more of these things than we are expecting,' he complained. 'They are making difficulties.'

Peter waited a moment, bending down to scratch at the dike with a loose rock. It scored easily under the granite. He stood up and asked, 'What were your expectations based on?'

The manager shrugged his shoulders, shouted something to the men with the drill steels. Thea was watching everything.

'It's just,' Peter said, 'that I was told there was no detailed geological survey available for this pluton.'

The man stared at him. They must have been about the same age and, as over the lunch table of two days before, Peter felt a definite affinity. And reticence too. As of friendly competitors in opposing teams, hiding their cards.

'On other quarries,' he said.

'Oh. I didn't realise there were others.'

Thea said quickly, 'The company has four quarries in this region.'

'Yes, we are basing our volume and speed calculations on production in those quarries.'

'But are they won from the same pluton?'

The quarry manager pursed his lips, as if to show he didn't understand. Peter repeated the question. But was interrupted by Thea who spoke for too long to be merely translating. Then she said, 'We don't know the exact geological details.'

'But the colour is the same?'

'There are eight colours on the island,' the manager said. 'All grey.'

Thea laughed. 'Eight shades of grey.'

'And when the Australians came to look, why did you bring them to this quarry?'

'It's the best.'

'But with more discontinuities than you expected.'

The manager smiled with a 'that's-life' shrug of the shoulders. As if all was now clear. It was nothing more than bad luck. They stood just a yard or two from a drop of perhaps forty feet into the quarry where the front loader was still fighting its block across the floor sending up clouds of diesel. To the east the sea wasn't so much visible as an understood presence, the hills sloping down to blueness, the inevitable beyond the horizon. He remembered yesterday evening's vision of its calm uniformity, silently embracing an island's complications. And the roar of the powerboat.

A dumper arrived to shift rubble from where the new line must pass. Beyond the cleared area, the vegetation above a weathered rock face was coarse grass and thyme, the dark, waxy leaves of shrubs. The air was quite still, the heat intensifying.

'Have you ever had trouble making up your volume?'

'All deliveries are on time, no?' The man laughed. 'Of course we are having trouble. But we overcome.'

'A lot of rock gets sent back.'

'Because they think it is bad when it isn't bad.'

'But what would you do,' Peter asked, 'if you couldn't make up the volume? The contract has fairly strong sanctions as I understand. It just seems extraordinary to me that you would sign it without a proper geological study.'

'I am not signing it me,' the quarry manager laughed.

'But if you couldn't make up your volume?'

'They fire me,' he laughed. With the index finger of his right hand he made one of those gestures that mean the same the world over; a knife cutting across the throat of the sacrificial victim.

'I thought they never fired anybody in these state-owned companies.'

The quarry manager was determined to make light. Or perhaps genuinely hadn't realised that the conversation was more than chatter. 'Because we always achieve our quota, no?'

Thea laughed. Then Peter said that he had asked to have the quarry manager at his disposal today because he wanted to show him something and hopefully solve a mystery. They clambered back down the steel ladder and walked across the quarry floor to the prefab.

———— • ————

The etymology of 'pluton' is all too plain. Pluto is the god of the underworld, of the dead. The pluton forms in the underworld at incandescent depths, to surface only after millions of years of erosion, cold, silent and hard, the way bones may surface as the flesh sinks beneath a lifetime's attrition, or the way a character, an idea, a god, emerges from the pages of an ancient text, emptied of whatever meaning once was, but always ready to be used again, incorporated in a new matrix, a poem, a painting, a tower block.

But Pluto also means, 'the rich one'. For what riches could be more formidable than the ranks of the dead, what harvest more secure from meteorological caprice than that of the grim reaper? Again the etymology is apt, for the pluton is rich too, rich in minerals and ornamental rocks, to be slabbed and sold, 'in every corner of the globe', as this supplier's literature would have it. In 1991 each square metre of polished grey pearl from the Palinu quarry was fetching a price of 121 US dollars.

Peter opened his case. The slab he lifted out had once been 1130 by 565 by 27 millimetres, but rather less than half the length had fallen from the supporting formwork. The bloodstain was along the jagged edge which must have made short work of Jerry Owen's cranium. When this was explained, Thea turned and left the prefab. An unexpected squeamishness. But it wasn't the blood Peter was interested in talking to the quarry manager about, so much as the grain size and orientation. Where had this slab come from? The quarry man immediately protested that he was not a geologist, but then was bound to admit the differences between this and the kind of rock they were pulling out now. However, there had been patches in the quarry, particularly at the beginning, that were finer grained.

Peter asked to be shown the corresponding quarry walls. The manager and Thea walked beside him. The sun on overalls was sweltering, and around the neck dust clung to sweat. He had brought his crack hammer from his bag and set about taking samples. The light flashed over its steel shaft. They were at the very mouth of the quarry. On the outside, vertically scored with drill-holes, the rock was weathered, darkened, already there were lichens clinging. But only a centimetre in, when he got to work with his hammer, the stone was fresh and clean. And it was immediately evident from the fragments he chipped away that the explanation was not to be found here, as he had known it could not be. Hints of different graining patterns there were, perhaps under a microscope one might find a different accidental, a speck of different colour declaring the interminable uniqueness of the rock, but the quartz crystals were always the same visible size, a dusting of snowflakes deep in the stone.

The quarry manager examined the specimens he produced and said nothing. Thea began to speak to him in their own language. The manager replied, presumably explaining the situation. Peter prised in a crack, aware of the puzzle of sounds whose arrangement he couldn't understand, the way he was a complete layman when it came to looking at the surface of a piece of wood, for example, or a leaf, or Maifredi's vases, which, oddly, he could still see in his mind's eye. Red and black profiles against a white background. The sculpted contours of Thea's face against noon light.

'Why have you kept the quarry development so narrow?' he interrupted, turning away from the rough wall. 'There's nowhere for the shock waves to escape. It damages the stone.'

Caught off guard, the quarry manager replied at once: 'Somebody of important is not wanting to disturb the view from that hill. A person is planning a villa. We must not open the hill at the left.'

Thea said quickly, 'The island has severe restrictions on the aesthetic impact of territorial development.' She smiled.

'Were the Australians informed of the way the quarry would be developed?' But before anybody could answer or even choose not to answer this, he went on: 'The next thing I'd like to do is see the colour-range samples mentioned in the contract.'

The quarry manager seemed relieved. 'For this you must return to the finishing plant. In the technical office.'

'And the other three quarries?'

'Do you want to visit?'

'Only if it is worth it.'

'The grey tone is completely different. I assure you.

But if you are feeling . . .'

They had arrived back at the prefab. A man was drumming his finger on the drinks dispenser, the pornography was motionless on the walls. With a corrugated-iron roof under intense sunlight, the air, despite open windows, trembled with heat. Before putting his crack hammer back in his bag, Peter said, 'Listen.' He lifted the half slab from the desk, stood it on the floor, and, holding it there with one hand, struck it sharply with his hammer. The tone was dull, but not entirely so. A faint ringing lingered in the hot air. The quarry manager stared and shook his head. 'Not so bad,' he said. And crouching down to look from an oblique angle, 'No microfractures also.'

'No, no microfractures,' Peter said.

Then, walking out of the prefab, they were met by the boom of an explosion. Channelled down the narrow walls of the quarry, the blast swept by them in a thick, warm wave. For a moment he was in another dimension, intensely aware, oneiric, almost hallucinating. He swayed, stumbled. He remembered the evil in the rock, the bow wave of the motorboat, Pluto's vase-bound horses rising from the underworld to carry off Persephone, in black silhouette against the light. As the blast subsided, he could feel the blood pulsing in his neck with a machine rhythm. His skin prickled with heat. And he thought how mindless and endless such associations were, an interminable clustering and dissolving, forming and re-forming. That extraordinary proliferation. Why should he insist so much on these details? To what end? He would go to bed with Thea again. He didn't care what her role was, what his destiny. Peter Nicholson was suddenly filled with a frothing intoxication.

———— • ————

This beautiful woman apparently liked to live in the half-dark. She had lowered the shutters so that only slats of light could enter, projecting themselves in a distorted grid on to ceramics: illite, smectite, chlorite and silica fired at over a thousand degrees. Her cool, bare feet trod a pattern where each square was interlocking rectangles of grey, white and serpentine green. Thus crossing from window to bed, her body was pale, almost luminous, and the jet black hair a barely seen aura round her head. She reminded him of no other woman. She had no gestures, as Hazel Owen did, evoking weeping wives, supermarket queues; no tenderness, that talent Margaret had for intimacy; nor any of suburbia's fertility and bitterness. Her conversation was not conversation, but, as it were, a constant making and breaking of contact, a forward and backward of tingling impulses, as though in some oscillating device to keep a machine in motion. She wouldn't talk shop. She didn't broach the subject of the slab. There seemed no subject at all to what she said, but tones of banter and challenge. And her accentless voice conveyed no character, unless it were a faintly ironic concealment of character. She was entirely foreign. He couldn't place her at all. To define her otherwise than by negatives you would have had to say, a perfect, palely-luminous body moving across the cool-tiled floor of a darkened room. Here, in this place that was nowhere to him. Carrying iced drinks. A padding and clinking. And there was a fly, too, bumping against the blind where the light was sliced and stacked.

It was at this particular moment that it first occurred to Peter he might never return to Barnet Hill, to that sad terrain whose future exploitation had become so problematic. Did he want to return? As she stretched out beside him, he had a feeling as if of falling. The cracks yawned. He seemed to float free. Then almost blacked out. 'A touch too much of sun,' he said. He must phone his wife as soon as he was out of here. It became important.

Love was made. His head began to clear. A mundane and rather squalid reality silted back. Which he felt safer with. Something of an old dog, in fact. Scoring. And this made him ask, to pass the time, 'Your Maifredi, he seemed a rather randy old so-and-so?'

The tinkling laugh. 'You mean the fact that he touched me every ten seconds.'

'Yes.'

'Doctor Maifredi is a very clever man.'

'I don't doubt it.'

There was a pause. 'But you want to know if I have been to bed with him.' Her voice was slightly abrasive.

'Oh, I'm not jealous.'

'You have no cause to be jealous. You have a woman of your own.'

Peter was silent for a moment. Presumably she meant his wife. Whom he had never mentioned having. Yet her choice of the word 'woman' seemed curiously out of keeping with her otherwise perfect English. Still, he could think of no cause to worry. He would be home all too soon.

'I was just surprised to see how familiar he was with you.'

'You mean gross?'

'Well, yes, you seem such opposites. I thought it odd him pawing you and then making dirty remarks when you went off to swim.'

They lay in the half-dark. He was aware of anxieties crowding now. One phoned one's wife, who one had so completely substituted it wasn't even her one was cheating on. Was this possible? Could he really just phone her and go back? It would seem more in keeping for Hazel Owen to phone her irreplaceable husband, or in some seance to ask him how the slab had fallen, and how it came to be a different slab. As if, found dead in bed with quite the wrong woman, they haunted your ghost to know why and who she was. But the sun had made him giddy. Drinks over an early lunch. A thousand changes of plan.

'From my appearance,' she insisted, 'do you think I'm the kind who would sleep with a man like that? To get my job, maybe?'

'I don't even know what your job is when you're not looking after me.'

'I run his life. He more or less runs the island.'

Peter said nothing. He hadn't realised the man was that important.

'So? Come on,' she taunted. 'What do you think? A fat, ambiguous politician who collects classical vases and likes stories of abduction, rape and sodomy with the perpetrator always in a divine or heroic role. Would I? My type? For mercenary reasons? What would somebody observing me think?'

Apparently it was a game. There was the note of challenge in her voice again. He found it grating, but knew he would rise to it all the same. By the window the fly buzzed wildly in and out of the knives of light. Then was silent.

'Well, you slept with me.'

'You are rather attractive, polite, well-mannered.' She paused: 'Innocuous.'

'Why thank you.'

'And there are no complications.'

'I should hope not.'

'But with a man with a paunch longer than his cock, gold teeth, bald, farting, a wife who does nothing but knit and whine on the phone to their children in other continents. What do you think?'

She was becoming aggressive. Inexplicably so. And in bad taste too.

'But you said he was clever.'

'A genius I think, actually.'

'And he is charming, in his way.'

'Intensely.'

'And a collector of beautiful objects.'

'People come a long way to see them.'

'Then you keep your swimming costume there. And your bathrobe. So you must go often.'

'I do.'

He was silent. He would have liked to change the subject. He would have liked to be back with Margaret.

'So? Would I?'

'How should I know?'

She was up on one elbow, a satirical smile on her face. 'By looking at me, at him. The way you're always looking at your rocks. To find out things.'

Peter said lightly, 'Of course I can't know if you have, but I suspect, well, I suspect you would.'

She sat up and slapped him hard round the face. It was a complete surprise. And painful. She stood up, found a dressing gown, shaking her head vigorously. 'How incredibly stupid you are. How blind. You're a baby. It's criminal.'

He dressed quickly and, at some point in the silent ride back to the hotel, took the envelope with the money from his breast pocket and laid it on the dashboard.

'This was given to me by mistake,' he said.

She didn't so much as look at it.

———— • ————

The thing about metamorphosis was that one was and wasn't what one had always been. The chemical elements were the same perhaps, but it was the deployment that mattered. When he thought of himself now and a year ago, Peter knew that identity was a hallucination, a convenient fiction. Yet people were predictable. A sort of shell remained: blue eyes, certain old habits. As though after intense metasomatism: same texture, same shape, different minerals. He might have known, for example, that Murray would still be out at lunch mid-afternoon. Peter called from the same booth in the hotel corridor. His secretary, Charlotte, was chatty, despite international charges: the weather, a burst water-main by the tube station. 'Tell him,' Peter said, 'I've got something absolutely damning. He should call me at once.'

Then he dialled his own phone and got the high-pitched invitation of the fax. Again he should have known. Anna would be collecting the children. Or she was refusing to speak to people again. More drama. So perhaps he could scribble something. But he knew he wouldn't. There was that inability to step back into his allotted square. It was almost physical. Walking through the lobby, he noticed Hazel's child, Wendy, sitting in one of the armchairs reading a comic book, and on impulse went to sit beside her. Again, he had the impression the girl was an ally. She understood.

'My little boy likes Asterix,' he told her. 'He's nine.'

'It's the one where they disguise themselves as trees,' she explained.

'Oh yes. And then jump on the centurion.'

'Legionary.'

'Ah. Where's your mum?'

'She said she was going out for the afternoon.' The girl kept her prim infant distance.

'And you're supposed to wait for her here?'

'Yes.'

'That's not much fun, is it?'

She looked at him. She had a soft, unformed, infant face, relaxed and wide eyed. The undifferentiated vitality still had to take on detail. The skin was still transparent, with nothing of the mother's hardness in her features.

Round her neck was a simple chain with a small green stone cut in characteristic droplet shape.

'Is that jade?' he asked.

She tucked her chin into her neck and lifted the stone from the V of her shirt. 'It's to chase off evil spirits,' she confided. 'Or that's what grandma said. It's magic. She gave it to me when I was born.'

'It's very nice. Real jade too. You're a lucky girl.'

He stood up. She was still lowering her eyes to try to look at her stone. 'Do you think it really can chase off evil spirits?'

He laughed. 'I'm not sure what evil spirits are.'

But the girl had no problem. 'Spirits that hurt you.'

'I'm not sure what spirits are.'

'They're dead people,' she informed him. Her tone was condescending now. He should have known.

'I don't quite see why dead people would want to hurt you. But the stone is beautiful.'

'Maybe when they see how beautiful it is, they don't want to hurt you any more.'

'Could be,' he said. 'Or perhaps they just realise how pointless it would be. Stones do that to you. They're so old, nothing means anything any more.'

She eyed him uncertainly. 'Then perhaps I should give it to Mummy?'

Peter looked at her. He sat down again. 'Why's that?'

She shrugged her shoulders, pulled a face in the cartoon way children will.

'Nobody wants to hurt your mummy. Least of all any dead person.'

Only when he said this did he think of the girl's father.

The girl opened and closed her legs. 'Mummy said if she didn't come back tonight, I should come and talk to you.'

'To me?'

'You're in Room Number 221, aren't you? With your

girlfriend. Mummy said you were having an affair.'

Peter had imagined a few utterly discreet days. Simple work, exciting sex. No complications, bar the prospect of re-entry. He said, 'But why did she think she might not come back?'

'Dunno.' The girl shrugged her thin shoulders.

'Well, what's she gone to do? I thought you were going back tomorrow.'

'Tomorrow evening.'

'And you don't know what she's doing?'

'She said she had to go and see someone.'

'About your father's accident?'

'I suppose so.'

'You don't know who?'

'No. Anyway, she might not really have gone to see anyone.'

'Oh?'

'Sometimes she just likes to walk about being unhappy.'

'Ah.'

'And then she doesn't like to have me around because she's thinking of Dad. She likes to just mope and think of Dad.'

'I see.'

'She says he calls to her.'

Peter drew breath. He asked, 'What if she were to find out who was actually responsible for the accident, what would she do?'

'She says she'll kill them.'

But Peter thought he frequently threatened to kill Mark and Sarah when they wouldn't quieten down for bed.

'How?'

The girl shrugged her shoulders. 'Mum's smart,' she said. 'Much more than Dad.' She pulled a face. 'I just hope she makes up her mind, so that we can go home.'

They were both silent a moment. There was a small buzz in the lobby as a guide checked out a group of

Scandinavians. Then the girl simply went back to her book. Turning a page, Asterix was underground now, in a maze of stalagtites where the Gauls had hidden their bizarre weaponry. 'If there's any problem at all, just knock on my door,' Peter said.

———— • ————

Peter sat in 221 holding a piece of paper. How even one's holidays from life took on a rhythm, tended to routine! He got up in the morning, was driven out to finishing plant or quarry, lunched, dallied with his interpreter, came back to the hotel, went out mid-afternoon to find Margaret at the rented sunshade on the beach: swimming, dinner, sex. Even if it was only for a few days, it was impossible to avoid the sense of process setting in. And there was an area of himself that was immensely pleased. Pleased with his capacity for action, for self-justification, for getting around. And another that was beginning to feel distinctly queasy, almost nostalgic for the old bedding plane, the days whose slow stillicide might have been millennia.

'Dear Peter,' he read. It was scribbled by hand. The lines were broken on the shiny paper where the fax had been unable to read them. Three pages.

'Do you remember when we went to the Lake District last year and it rained and rained and you went out and bought that thousand-piece jigsaw of the San Francisco earthquake and kept the kids busy for two whole days so that they didn't even want to go out when the rain stopped. I thought about it this morning and remembered how much I loved you for doing that, for making them happy that time, since I would never have the patience, and how funny it was that a quiet, meticulous man like you would choose a subject like an earthquake.

'Peter, it is now two days since I faxed you the news

that we are expecting a third child. Naturally I imagined you would phone immediately. I even hoped you would be delighted. You have always been such a good father. I hoped you would be loving and we could get back to being two warm little bunnies again and forget the awful coldness of this last year, which has been quite stupid when you think about it. There was no reason for it. There is no reason that I can see why we can't be perfectly happy now. Peter, think how lovely it could be. Don't let's spoil everything.

'Otherwise, if you don't phone, if you imagine I can simply be put off while you "concentrate on your job", if you use your patience and meticulousness to hide from me, then I shall go straight out and get myself an abortion. I'm already eleven weeks on.

'ANNA.'

It was extraordinary, Peter thought, that she could write, 'this last year', not sensing that the incline had been downwards for a decade, was the very shape of their relationship. There had been a choice of horses nuzzling together by a river, a stately house with ivies, rhododendrons and a gilded carriage, and the earthquake. Of course he chose the earthquake.

Not that he didn't see the lure of it: her bunny talk, its animate snugness. Just that there was a way in which he wasn't sad about being unhappy now. It was destructive, but there you are. And stretching out, eyes closed, on the bed, waiting for Murray to return his call, it occurred to him that men and women were perhaps always at cross purposes here. One needed them for some reason. But not, as they, and sometimes you, imagined, for themselves. No, there was always some getting on to be done, of which they were the vital catalyst. Their magic helped you slay some monster, become something else. But then it was a new monster you were after and a new magic you needed. With a clarity of polarised light through crossed-

Nichols, he saw that Margaret had been the sharp edge he needed to cut through the coils of some petrified coward in himself. And Thea a sort of mirror in which to stare at his new self, to watch himself flex his muscles, to double his image in delightful vertigo. While the chameleon monster, perhaps, this creature who could never be slain often enough, was routine: the interminable mechanical clank slabbing the rock, the breakfast table laid before going to bed, the children's sandwiches prepared and waiting in the fridge, the Saturdays, Sundays and family holidays, year in, year out, that chequered pattern eating up every empty space, through four dimensions, and the blades descending millimetre by millimetre, hour by hour, through the evil in the heart of the rock, till the limit-switch tripped, a bell rang and it was over. The block was so many identical tombstones.

The bell rang. He hadn't known he was asleep. So overwhelming was his angst upon waking that he was paralysed in a slime of sweat and strange lights behind the eyes. The room fell into place as if from a great height, as if powered down by the ruthless beam of sunlight that skewered its banality so sharply. He was utterly disorientated.

While the measured trill of the phone confirmed right-angles, utilitarian furniture, man-made geometry, enclosed spaces, the back and forth of electronic conversation. It must be Murray, his work, his identity.

———— • ————

'Hello?'

He failed to recognise the voice at first. Its ironic intimacy was baffling.

'Peter.'

'Oh, Thea. Hello.'

There was an awkward pause.

'You said you wanted availability of our test equipment. I was phoning to confirm you can examine or use the equipment any time you want, as long as you give us a couple of hours' warning. The colour range samples are available on request in the safe of the design office above the finishing plant. You can also see all the shear, modulus of rupture and modulus of compression certificates from the Universities of Athens, Pisa and Sydney.'

'Thank you.' He hesitated. 'I thought I'd come in tomorrow morning. There was a spot of sightseeing I wanted to do this afternoon.'

She laughed. 'How formal we are.'

'As I remember, we didn't leave each other on the best of terms.'

'No,' she said. 'I slapped your face.'

He waited, still dazed by the way afternoon reverie had turned to nightmare. A glance at his watch showed half an hour had passed. He was late for Margaret. Then he heard her saying: 'Your naivety is beginning to get on my nerves.'

He cast about. 'I'm in a foreign country. Did I do something wrong?'

Again, her smoke-screen was laughter. 'You forgot to call me "Madam".'

'But only a moment ago you accused me of being too formal.'

She said, 'You shouldn't have given me the envelope back. That was stupid.'

There was another long silence. Peter was aware of how quickly he had got out of his depth. Floundering, he tried to bluff. 'It would have been dishonest of me to do otherwise. Clearly it wasn't meant for me. Anyway, there was no covering letter.'

She said, 'You're being ridiculous.'

Exasperated, he told her people didn't do things like this where he came from.

'But you do have a fling with your interpreter.'

'That's a different business altogether.'

Very slowly and coolly, she said, 'Perhaps where you come from it is. But you're not at home now.'

'Look,' he took a deep breath to overcome anxiety, 'if you've got something you phoned to tell me, then let's hear it. Otherwise I've got a busy day ahead, thank you very much.'

'Peter Nicholson.' He sensed how she at once caressed and ironised his name. After a pause she finished, 'We were making love only an hour ago.'

He was disturbed by the truth of that simple observation, and at the same time fleetingly aware that telephone calls could perfectly well be recorded. And they were in a Mediterranean country with a great deal of money at stake. Had there been any need, for example, to actually show them the stone?

'Perhaps I have been rather naive,' he sighed. 'You may be right.'

She was immediately cheerful, as though with a child who has decided to see reason. 'Not to worry. There's no reason why anything should come of it. I'll see you tomorrow morning. The driver will be there at the usual time.'

'Thanks.'

'And Peter.'

'Yes?'

'You remember you asked me about where I came from and so on and so forth?'

'Yes.'

'Perhaps it was disingenuous of me. I should have said that Dr Maifredi is my father.'

Peter remembered the bright sunlight, the serrated detail of the house, the intensity of colour martialled into squares and rectangles, polished stone, polished skin. How enigmatic all that clarity turned out to be.

He must be more careful.

'And I hope we can meet after lunch again tomorrow. It will be your last day, won't it?'

'Yes. That would be nice.'

No sooner had he got the phone down than it was trilling away again, as if not wanting to let him off the hook so easily. He reached out his hand, but then decided against. He felt shaken, and not exactly sure on what footing he had left things. Perhaps it would be a mistake to tell Murray. He must decide. Changing into shorts and T-shirt, he left the room.

A few minutes later he was back. He removed Hazel Owen's slab from its case and looked about the room. But it couldn't be hidden here. He went out into the corridor. There was a cleaning cupboard, a trolley. Too obvious. He took the lift to the top floor and climbed the inevitable stairs that led to the roof. An iron door was loosely bolted. He left the slab outside leaning innocently against a low parapet.

———— • ————

One suddenly developed a sense of how long life was, the appropriateness of that length, one's position along a curve whose trajectory had become clear. Around his fortieth birthday it happened. Perhaps on that train, reading the brief about the fugitive watercourse. And you felt you were in control, the way in a race, or difficult task, there comes that moment when you realise you can pace yourself through to the end. The curve was clear enough now. It could be projected to its conclusion. The continents had drifted so much and would drift so much more. Perhaps, in layer after layer of contributions, a pension was taking shape. The sedimentary life. It was rather gratifying, it was reassuring. And utterly, utterly frustrating. Why draw in a line that was already there?

Margaret wasn't at the sunshade. He walked down to the sea and looked out. Bathers splashed and cried. In their hundreds. Coloured balls flew. Sprays of water sparkled fearfully. Shattered light and detail. Then the flat, undifferentiated distance beyond, melting to blue nothingness, only the cone of the volcano gathering the horizon. Suddenly he felt he must see the volcano.

He turned. At the water's edge a boy and girl had built a sandcastle: extensive ramparts, crenellated ranks of sand-pies. But the tide had turned and water was lapping around it now. The outer wall reached saturation point. The surface tension couldn't hold, the angle of repose gave. A great chunk of sand slithered down into the sea. But this was no more than the children wanted. Furiously, their spades repaired the damage. Their shrill voices screamed defiance. They dug canals to drain the sea away. They threw up brave walls. The sea lapped forward with quiet insistence. The outer ramparts again returned to muddy flatness. Giggling and sand-bespattered, they lay down their bodies to save the crumbling keep, their hands scooping and scooping the sand. Peter watched, thinking of his own precious children, how they held him to them, how bonds formed and dissolved on every side, and how sandcastles are always best when built on the precarious margin of the sea: the sun-drenched detail dissolving in froth, the advancing wavelets reflecting an empty sky.

A hand tapped him on the shoulder. Margaret's pearly face was cocked to one side. 'Somebody gave me this envelope for you. I went up to the café to try and phone.'

As they walked away, he turned and saw the children on their feet now. They had sensed what the end must be and were trampling down what was left of their masterpiece, to get it before the sea did. Peter saw their exultation as they kicked down all their patient building, their faces savage and joyous.

'I told him it was silly, leaving it here with me when the hotel was only ten minutes away.'

They walked across the hot, white, cleanly-sieved sand toward the sunshades. Turning the package over, Peter saw they had merely sellotaped over where he had previously opened it. Thea must have known even as she spoke to him.

'Who left it?'

'A man. Young. Quite nice. I told him it was silly, but he didn't speak any English.'

'Can I put it in your handbag?'

'Aren't you going to open it?'

'I know what's inside.' Obviously the call had been to make sure he accepted this time. To show it was no joke. To say that she was Maifredi's daughter. Not a disinterested interpreter.

He sat on his deckchair and they stared at each other. Her eyes searched. His simply stared. The extraordinary complicity of that first gaze across the British Rail compartment four months ago was lost now. There were things he wasn't telling her.

'What is it?' she asked.

'I don't feel like swimming this afternoon. The sun's got to me.'

She stared at him. She was too perceptive.

They walked the beach to the little port and caught one of the small launches that plied tourists back and forth among the islands. The trip was an hour and a half. Late afternoon. She sat by his side under the shade of an awning as they watched the hard-etched land shrink and darken behind the froth of their wake. With that remarkable patience she had, she waited, as one who knows the other will eventually speak without prodding or prompting. Finally he said, 'I was lying yesterday when I told you I'd phoned my wife. I haven't phoned her at all.'

'Oh, and so?'

'So nothing. I'm getting mixed up. Too much is going on. When you said it was over, after we got back, it was as if I couldn't care less any more. About anything. I saw my life so clearly, how everything will always be, I didn't want it any more. I'd rather the mess.'

He seemed to have invented this truth even as he uttered it. Speech can be dangerous like that. He banged a fist on the empty seat in front. 'God, I can't imagine a more mixed-up situation.'

'It seems perfectly simple to me. We have a good time now. Then we go back. First we have fun, then we suffer.'

That brutal clarity younger people have. Though there was a gentleness in her voice.

He lifted his eyes to look. How could she be worked into the prosaic trajectory of that curve that was his life? What would the shape be then? But trying to imagine had the same painfulness of prodding one's brain for a lost dream. Or a calculation that refused to come out. He bit the inside of his cheek. 'You know why that man left the envelope at the sunshade with you, rather than at the hotel? To show me that they know about you.' He explained there was money in the envelope. They wanted him to write an accommodating report.

Understandably, it was a few moments before she took this in.

'So it *is* all their fault.'

'Not necessarily, it may be a perfectly normal way of doing things in this part of the world. Oiling the wheels. I don't know. It's not that much money. They just suppose it will make things easier. But like I said, they were also showing me they knew about you. And that they can play on that knowledge.'

She was silent a moment. The truncated cone of the

volcano had begun to loom now, taller and steeper than it had seemed. The lava slopes had a sparse, austerely primitive vegetation and above the sea-line you could glimpse great holes and caves that had been gassy bubbles, blown out through the molten rock.

'What are you going to do?'

'What do you think I should do?'

Her full lips were pursed in thought. 'Would it be hard to write an accommodating report?'

'On the contrary. I just make a lot of small criticisms that don't carry any weight: the attitude of the workers, the presence of microfractures. All they have to do is demonstrate that other customers are happy and they're fine.'

'But is there anything else you want to put in the report that should be in there?'

He explained about the slab.

'Hazel is right then. Somebody was responsible for the accident.'

But he said that was jumping the gun. There could still be a perfectly simple explanation. A block from another quarry for another job had accidentally been cut for the Marlborough Place job, for example. Or seeing they were getting behind schedule, the building contractors had bought from another source.

'Wouldn't it be important to establish which? Seeing that it actually killed this bloke.'

'Tomorrow I'll try and see how strong the stone is. They've got some testing equipment. Perhaps it's just as strong as the other. In which case the question of where it came from is irrelevant.'

Peter knew this could not be true. But it was also possible that they didn't know. And likewise that this second offer of the money had nothing to do with the slab. In any event, it was fortunate Murray had been out when he called. Nothing had been decided yet.

'The bottom line is,' she said, 'that you think that if you start putting all that in the report, they might tell Anna about me. They might blackmail you.'

He noticed how she used his wife's name in such a familiar way. He paused. 'Maybe. But perhaps that's exactly what I want. I would be free. It would be a *fait accompli*.'

'No. If you want to tell her, you tell her yourself,' she said.

He felt rebuked. She had never spoken to him like that. To make matters worse, he still hadn't explained the half. The lattice was far more complex, the equilibrium more precarious. He himself was someone else.

Desperately, but soft, he said, 'I love you, Margaret. I have never felt so simply myself with anyone but you.' This was true.

She smiled and embraced him. There was the smell of her hair, her sun-warm skin. His back was against the railing over the dark sea as the boat slowed now and prepared to manoeuvre into port. For some reason then he remembered the children and their sandcastle, how savagely they had stamped on it.

Finally she detached herself. 'In the end it's you who has to decide. Don't torture yourself about it. Just do as you feel you should, in your heart.'

But Peter said he didn't have a heart any more. It had fractured into three, four, five parts. Too much shear. Though the largest part wanted her. And he led her into the mill of the passengers gathering round the gangway.

———— ● ————

Over the years he had built up quite a handsome rock collection. As a teenager, he would cycle out to quarries or roadworks, keep an eye open for landslips and rockfalls. Perhaps that was the beginning of his ordered life. You took mallet, hammer and chisel in your knapsack. Anna sat making the sandwiches and begged him to be careful. His eye ran across the rock face, looking for something interesting, a tell-tale change of colour. Or he was staring at heaps of rubbled breccia, kicking the rocks aside to pick out ammonite fragments. And it wasn't possession that mattered, so much as discovery and identification, which put you in a special relationship with the world. An easy mastery. He hammered at the hard, red Devonian limestones north of Plymouth, the black Hoptonwood Stone of Derbyshire, brought back a fine piece of marble from Northern Ireland, a speckled green eclogite from Gleneig. On the Isle of Skye a splinter of skarn took a chunk out of his cornea. That was their honeymoon.

You carried the rocks home and chiselled them into parallelopipeds, ten by five by three centimetres. He kept the two larger surfaces flat, bevelling the edges in such a way that the hammer blows would not show. And if the texture would take a polish, he polished it. Then each specimen was classified according to location, age and genesis, before being placed on the velvet background of his specimen cases. There were a few dozen such cases stacked in the third bedroom, which served as his study. When the children upset them all over the carpet, he had no difficulty putting them back in order again. His mind spanned the hundreds of millions of years, the thousands of mineral combinations, so readily. And in the sitting room there was a glass-topped display case with his finest trophies: polished Larvikite like a block of blue ice from a trip to Norway, a deep red Griquaite from South Africa, a particularly bubbly travertine from Lazio. But those were the adventurous holidays before the children arrived. The last specimen he had collected was nothing better than a small pyritised fossil in mesozoic limestone.

Showing it to Margaret in the railway compartment that day, still freshly cut and spiky, he had likened it to himself. A modest mollusc of times past.

'How long have we got?' he asked, as she consulted the timetable posted on the quay.

'Last boat departs nine-thirty. Three hours.'

'It's a geologist's paradise,' he said, looking up at the frozen lava flow. But he didn't regret his mallet and chisel. He hadn't made the trip for that. Though he could think of no other reason. From the quay a road had been carved out between mountain and sea round to where erosion had allowed a flatter area to form. A church was prominent. The houses were simple cubes, built, no doubt, in the light, air-filled extrusive rock of the volcano, then stuccoed white, topped in hard-baked terracotta. The steep slopes and sharp twists of the valley hadn't allowed for the triumph of straight lines, but a higgledy-piggledy accumulation, at once gay in clear sunshine and precariously huddled. Hikers could be seen with their colourful backpacks on the looming slopes above, where the profile of the truncated cone had to be imagined now. Grey scars of tuff outcropped everywhere through a thin soil cover, and entering the village a notice in four languages warned that drinking water on the island had to be brought from the mainland. The first poky shop window displayed souvenir volcanoes carved in peperino. Everything, it seemed, was conditioned by that violent explosion that had last re-shaped the place some four hundred years ago.

'I hope it's extinct,' Margaret laughed. They struck up a path, climbed for perhaps half an hour. To their right the sea lay calm and flat under the intense heat of the sun, though this was slanting now, so that the fissure in a patch of exposed lava at their feet was shaded black against the silver grey of the stone. But then the slope steepened, the path narrowed, became rugged and her sandals were unsuitable. 'No can do,' she said. 'I'm sorry.'

For about ten minutes they stood on what was little more than a ledge above the sea and beneath the towering rock that had stoppered up pressure beneath for so long. The colours were dark, glassy-blue below, lighter blue above, and around them an infinite mottling of streaky greys and greens. A smell of thorny vegetation drifted up into the great wash of air where gulls hung. They stood arm in arm, on this ledge, above this stoppered gap in the earth's crust, and he would have liked to tell her that these volcanoes were famous for their pegmatites, and that he had sometimes thought of their love like that, a squeezing of all life's rich volatiles into one fabulous dike bursting through a waste of tuff. But she seemed to be thinking her own thoughts.

Coming down, he remembered the girl, Wendy, with her jade pendant waiting alone in the lobby. Where had Hazel Owen gone this time? And he thought, even though Murray had not been in, all the same he had told Charlotte he was on to something big. So it was unclear whether his colours were already nailed to the mast or not. The problem was arriving at that decision. For if circumstances should force him to make a stand, he had no doubt he would, whatever the cost. He had no trouble at all seeing himself plunge into an angry sea after a drowning child, or snatching someone from a burning building. It was arriving at that point of exposure he found so difficult. Usually there were so few reasons for risking one's neck.

They pressed themselves against the rock to let a line of Germans go by. The path was narrow and the coarse texture of the tuffaceous surface uncomfortable through thin shirts. Their hands sweated together, a hundred-foot drop just a step, a suicide pact away. When they were walking again he said, 'There are never these long silences with Anna. She talks all the time. Just like she sends faxes all the time. Meals are a constant barrage.'

The girl smiled.

He asked her what she was thinking of.

'The day, the sun,' she said.

But his own mind was racing desperately, an exasperation the volcano hadn't solved at all. It was he might erupt. 'I mean,' he protested, 'do you think it's right for her to blackmail me like this, saying she'll abort if I don't show some sign of commitment?'

Margaret had stopped to tie back her hair. There was the elegant lopsidedness of her features and a mole in the deep hollow of her neck. She was eighteen years younger than him.

'I suppose she just doesn't want to have the child if you're not happy together. I can see that.'

'Okay. So then I'm forced really to write an accommodating report for these people so as to save my wife from aborting.'

She laughed. 'Don't be ridiculous, Peter.'

'But I'm not. I said they brought that money to you to show me they knew about you. Then they've twice mentioned the fact I'm married. Very pointedly. I thought it was odd until now.'

'Calm down.'

'But how can I be calm?' At the same time as he said this, he was perfectly aware that almost all his angst was generated by the fear they would tell Margaret about Thea. Not Anna about Margaret. How could he claim to love her and then have sex with someone else? 'This is a farce, a pantomime' – he was beginning to speak very quickly – 'I'm being forced to make the most impossible decisions. I'll just have to write them the report they want and have done.'

They were approaching the houses again now and there were men spreading nets over a low wall. She stopped him so that they turned to look at each other.

'Peter,' she said. 'Don't link everything together like this. If you honestly believe the slab was responsible and it's somebody's fault, then say so. That's your job.'

Her voice was as cream to a sore, but it wasn't enough this time. Because he hadn't shown her where the real sore was. 'So I write a damning report,' he insisted, 'though I'm not even sure yet, and they tell Anna, and she goes crazy and aborts. And I'm responsible. The fact is things are linked.'

'Then separate them.'

'How?'

It was the closest they had come to arguing. Or at least he sensed an unpleasant belligerence and frustration in his own voice. Which was his inability to say what he must.

She said, 'You write an honest report. In the remote event, and it seems pretty unlikely to me, of their telling your wife about me, you admit that it's true and talk about your future. If she decides to abort, the decision is hers.'

'And you?' he said quietly, though he didn't even know what he wanted her to say.

'Me what?'

'Well . . .'

'Keep me separate, too,' she said. 'And if at that point you decide you want to be with me, let me know by registered letter and I'll give the question my prompt consideration.'

He thought, the people on each side of him were so sure of themselves, so definite. He was just that space between. And trapped there.

Seeing his face, she laughed. 'Peter, I can't see why you're so worried, sweetheart, when I have my bloody exam results to get back to.' Her slim arm round his waist squeezed, making him acutely aware how young she was, how sensibly cheerful.

They walked back. In the village church a votive painting showed a clipper foundering in a streak of lightning, while a blue-veiled Madonna reached down through storm clouds to protect the drowning crew. There were fresh flowers and candle smoke before an altar that must be the same pearl grey granite of the Talava pluton. 'Anna goes to church now,' he said, and when the girl's lightly tanned fingers came to rest on the polished wood of the altar rail, he almost took some awesome decision. Then a man in a cassock came to complain that their arms were bare.

They killed twenty minutes over a glass of wine behind the bead curtain of a shabby bar. He had a feeling of how this trip might have been: relaxing, sexy, inconsequential. There was a small museum at the end of the quay and looking at their watches they paid for tickets that were no more than a biro cross on a small scrap of paper. Inside were schoolroom models of the volcano, a centuries-old corpse preserved in some protected space beneath the lava, household implements from before Christ, a spoon, a pestle, fragments of pottery, examples of volcanic ash, obsidian, lapilli, pyroclastic blocks and bombs. The corpse was small and huddled in his stony skin, the face only a mask of death, as Thea's face in love-making had seemed a mask of life. One of the pottery fragments had a black-on-white design of a woman in exquisite profile. The line of nose and lips seemed to float free on that empty whiteness, as if part of nothing, cut free from the world and all its complications, whole. Whereas he was still in the state where things were constantly changing, things beyond control, like oneself, for which one was nevertheless responsible, in a way no mineral or slabbed stone, however treacherous, could be. And in his mind he had already gone back to the phone call, to Murray, to the envelope they had merely taped over, now once again in his pocket.

———— • ————

They were leaning on the guardrail of the boat again. Late evening. The foam beneath them churned and glowed in the dark light. Then she was kissing him softly on the neck when a voice beside them coughed. Maifredi had a fat smile, an incongruous presence, his heavy paunch loosely encompassed by white shirt and jacket. He waved a half-smoked cigar.

'I'm happy you find some time to enjoy, Mr Nicholson. I was afraid your duties would not have left so much space.'

He turned to Margaret with a small bow followed by a lift of smoke-wreathed eyebrows. His forehead in the diffuse evening light was beaded with sweat, despite a breeze from the prow. Peter introduced them. Maifredi knew how to say, 'Charmed, I'm sure.' Still looking at the girl, he said, 'A shame. I would to have taken you round the museum myself. The best pieces are not on sight: two vases of Melian inspiration.' He chuckled.

Politely, Margaret asked why they were not on show.

'Is always so here,' Maifredi smiled and puffed. The breeze snatched the smoke away. 'What is important is not on show. Or not where you await it. There is the farewell of Amphiaraus departing for Thebes and the sacrifice of Polyxena. I photographed them to make copies.' He patted a large camera case on his hip.

'I'm afraid I study economics,' Margaret said wryly.

'Ah, how sad,' he breathed. 'The older myths are so much more beautiful.' He hadn't taken his eyes off her. 'But wise, I think in this world.' He turned to Peter. 'Or not, Mr Nicholson?'

'Economics wouldn't be my choice. But then I have never been famous for my wisdom.'

The fat man chuckled throatily, presumably taking this as an allusion. 'Oh I'm certain that is not true, Mr Nicholson. I am certain you are very wise.' He laughed loudly, then coughed. 'And on that side, Thea says me you are happy with everything. You have what you need.' His fat fingers were constantly twitching the cigar, tapping out ash, lifting it to his mouth. As before, everything drew attention to his heavy physicality. 'Yes, yes, yes, everything will arrange itself very quick now, I am sure.'

'I'll finish tomorrow, or the day after.'

'Ah, that long.' Again a quizzical raising of the eyebrows, a knowing smile. 'Then you go back to your home?'

'Yes,' Peter said.

One hand jingling change in his pocket, paunch thrust out, Maifredi turned to the girl. His sleazy jollity contrived to be at once disarming and distasteful: 'This has been a good holiday, I hope, for the young lady. You have enjoyed very much.'

'Wonderful,' she said. 'I've spent most of the time on the beach.'

He almost giggled. 'Any time you wish to holiday again here, you two, you know, I'm sure we can do some arrangement for you. Then you can see those splendid vases at my house.'

'The copies, you mean,' Peter said.

Maifredi sighed smokily and shook his head, but his eye twinkled. 'I should not have told you so. It is so hard to distinguish them. Amphiaraus goes to his death so nobly!' Tossing his cigar over the rail, the fat man turned and went back to the saloon.

Margaret shivered. 'I see what you mean. That guy looks like he could bribe an army!'

But Peter didn't want to talk about it.

They stood at the rail. The sea was dark now, and with

the darkness it shared a sublime and massive monotony. There was a communion there. All around, the water and the night were lost in each other, utterly undifferentiated, while the pin-points of light growing brighter as they approached were the land, the sharp lines and curves of the land, constantly quarried and remoulded, shape after shape after shape: headlights carving out an olive grove, a patterning of yellow squares in a four- or five-storey block, necklaces of street-lamps draped over the hills. The boat's engine seemed to beat louder and more evenly as they rounded a promontory and turned into the bay. Peter and Margaret stood arm in arm at the prow enjoying a curious blend of relaxation and tension in each other's company.

'What if we stayed here for ever?' he suddenly said, 'If we never went back?'

But the girl only laughed.

The clock in the lobby told them half past eleven. With relief he noticed that young Wendy wasn't there. But over the granite desk, a man told him there had been phone calls: his company, and someone who hadn't wanted to leave her name. Telling Margaret to go to their room, he took the lift to the top floor and climbed the last flight of steps to the roof. But the iron door leading out was locked now. He shook it, then came downstairs again.

She was showering. At nearly midnight he turned on his computer and typed rapidly:

'Whereas the granite, strictly adamellite, examined to date, was found to have experienced no significant shearing *in situ* and could not be described as foliated (only a small percentage of the quartz was strained, and that only weakly), the failed stone alleged to have been the cause of the accident which brought about first a delay in the progress of the façade and ultimately a redesigning of the GRC formwork with all the attendant and considerable costs, showed marked foliation of the kind that might be associated with the metamorphic aureole, and which would undoubtedly weaken the rock, most notably in the vulnerable area of the drill-hole throats. Attempts to find comparable specimens from the quarry walls proved unsuccessful. Immediate checks should be carried out to establish whether other examples of the inferior rock have been installed on the building and in what circumstances. It should be observed that the specimen we examined displayed less microfracturing than slabs won from Talava, presumably because it had less pressure to unload, and thus to an unpractised eye might appear sounder than the Talava rock. It is the author's opinion that this anomalous rock would, in the right circumstances, be perfectly suitable for cladding as polished slabs, but not in the very large dimensions established in the original design of the Marlborough Place façade, and only using the traditional top-and-bottom ledge fixings, not side fixings with vulnerable drill-holes.'

He stared at the screen. One had a definite feeling of power writing it down. The power of one who knows, who analyses, whose conclusions cannot be disputed. And he thought, perhaps in the end a gesture like this could free him from private shock, poignant letters, the embarrassment and residual affection that breeds paralysis. Give himself to work. Fleetingly he was aware that for days he had deliberately repressed all thoughts of the children.

Leaning forward, fingers flying, he added, 'In the event of other and similar slabs of this variety being found on the building (particularly where serving as spandrel panels), this author would have to recommend immediate removal.'

Coming out of the bathroom, she said, 'Do you know, that's the first time we've ever spoken to anybody as a couple, the first time you've introduced me to anybody.

I mean, I know he's rather sleazy, but in a way I could have kissed him.'

There was a night cream she put on which immediately made him aware of her body, conjured the promise of unlimited discovery. So that again he said, 'But really, what if we never went back, if we just stayed here. Or elsewhere.' He felt desperately sentimental, clutching at straws. 'And I could introduce you to everybody.'

But she was already kissing his neck below the ear, slim fingers unbuttoning the top of his shirt. They were into their routine. Before the plane back, her exam results, her world.

Day Five
Morning

He had his petrographic microscope and was doing a point count to establish the mode. With his specimen sliced down to 30μ the light beneath came through in a grey glow, breaking into colour around stray accessories. His children took it in turns to look through the second eyepiece, and he was apologising profusely to them for the complexity and fragility of the matrix, its unpredictability. To make matters worse, there was a man's face that kept surfacing among the crystals and whose nose followed the specimen's main microfracture through a line of quartz grains to end abruptly against feldspar. But the children were reacting well, asking all the right questions – what was that orange bit, that thing that looked like glass? – though unfortunately they had to shout because of the din of the gangsaws from elsewhere in the building. Mark's voice was especially shrill.

He moved the specimen slightly, hoping this would get rid of the face, but it simply shifted, re-formed, grinning foolishly now, a skull-like grin, the eyes two black biotites and below a chipped tooth of white quartz. Sarah giggled. Mark fought over the lens to have a look. So that he had lost his place in the point count. He would have to go back to the beginning. He tried to adjust the analyser to make the face disappear, while explaining that the whole earth was made up of such combinations of minerals, or others similar, or others similar again, and the variations were endless. See how the vitreous quartz grains clung together, and then the background mass of the feldspars with the one microcline phenocryst that gave that porphyritic texture. And you had to think, normally this pattern, if you could call it that, would all be in three dimensions, and every single relationship – this crystal attached to the one above more strongly than to the other below – every single relationship and chemical formula played its part in determining the strength of the whole, so that you could never quite compute such a thing, but only break each randomly sectioned piece to find out.

Then he realised Margaret was in the room, cross-legged and quite naked in an executive chair, watching, smiling; but no, it was Thea, it was Thea, and the smile on that too-perfectly-chiselled face was a smile of challenge. She must have left a door open coming in because the noise of the slabbing was louder than ever and he was having to shout himself hoarse, but he must keep the children interested, otherwise they would turn and see her and they must not see her. They must not know about his other life.

Mark was at the eyepiece now. So, he shouted, it was all rather a muddle, but wasn't it beautiful too: those vivid patches of green, for example, traces of amphibole, each unique in shape and situation, not like man-made things, plastic and steel which were always the same right through. And still the face in the matrix wouldn't go away. Quite apart from anything else, how could he count the points and establish the mode when instead of intercepting grains of mica and feldspar the mode line seemed to be following the pores of this man's death-grey cheeks? A rusty patch of weathered magnetite looked like an old bloodstain where the groundmass was his hair. It was infuriating. But you had to establish the mode, children, which meant the relative percentages of the different minerals in the stone, you had to establish it so as to classify the stone and have an idea of its properties, so that you could then introduce it into the world of gangsaws and polished cladding, imposing the necessary order of gridwork stretching off into infinity, longitude and latitude, the composite kitchens of happy marriages, the city streets, the generations, the gravestones.

'Why are you leaving Mummy?' Sarah demanded abruptly and angrily. 'Why? Just when she has another little brother in her tummy for us.' His voice froze in his throat. He couldn't speak. Why? She screamed. The gangsaws roared. Why? The little girl kicked savagely at his ankles. He was going to go mad or explode. All kinds of scalding substances were rising within him. She kicked and kicked. Why?

'Peter,' another voice called. 'Peter!' So it *was* Margaret. The children must have seen. And the light beneath the specimen seemed to have grown brighter now, and the noise even louder, that unbearable screeching back and forth of steel in granite. He pressed his eye fiercely into the eyepiece to count the last few points of his line. He must concentrate on his work. Must must must. But the colours were almost washed out by the over-intense light now, the web of boundaries between mineral and mineral was dissolving, and with it that infuriating face, which he saw, just as it was lost in the glare, was Jerry Owen's.

Margaret had turned on the bedside lamp. She whispered, 'Peter, there's someone at the door.'

The pressure of light was transformed into the perfunctory detail of the room, the thundering gangsaws were only a handle fiercely rattling and fists banging against the door. He stood up, slithered over scattered clothes on the tiles, and when he turned the key, the little Australian girl simply tumbled into his arms.

———— • ————

Pluto is not the only god associated with the rock. There

is also the Christ rock, the Rock of Ages, foundation stone of the Church, a church which had included, since some four years ago, his wife. Anna had joined St Barnabas – neo gothic in a shelly Portland Roach – a short while after their regular love-making had ceased. There were distinct bivalve fossils dotted about the architrave and she took communion kneeling on diorite steps. So that in her faith, as in the way she rummaged in her handbag and approached conversations with a sort of square-jawed determination not to have the worst, Anna was not unlike the Australian woman, Hazel Owen, who had also spoken to him of her belief in God and in justice as defences against a selfish, mechanised world bent on realising investment at whatever human cost (as he presumably could be accused of realising himself at the expense of a life that hadn't yet begun). But God was not easily encouraged to intervene, and now, in her attempt to force His hand in her forlorn cause, to smite rivers of justice from that obstinate Christ rock, Hazel Owen was out there somewhere in this Mediterranean night, lost perhaps, perhaps injured. Was she the person who had tried to call him earlier in the evening? Wendy had fallen asleep in front of the TV in her room, then at four o'clock in the morning had woken up to find she was on her own. Mother hadn't come back.

'She said I should come to you, you would know what to do.'

Margaret dressed. They looked in the fridge and found a can of Coke for the child. Then, aware of the staleness in the room, Peter opened the window and pushed out the shutters. The square below languished in the sickly yellow with which we illuminate the night, but the small, human figure in marble above the little fountain got a white spotlight, and thus stood ghostly in the volume of fresh air moving through the streets.

'Did she go to the finishing plant?' he asked.

The girl shook her head. She didn't know. Before falling asleep she had changed herself into Micky Mouse pyjamas. There was the small, slim vulnerability Peter knew so well. Remembering his dream, he removed a pack of contraceptives from the bedside table.

'Or the quarry?'

'I don't know, she didn't say.'

Margaret gave the girl some sweets she had in her handbag and sat down beside her on the bed.

'She didn't say anything. Only for me to come and see you. She said you would know what to do.'

The girl ate her chocolate, drank her Coke. Peter could see the bump of the jade under her pyjama top. When she began to shiver, Margaret put an arm round her. The girl burst into tears. She wanted to go home. She didn't want to be here. She didn't care what had happened to Daddy or whether anybody should be punished for it. 'Mummy says she knows she's going to see him again and how she can feel his presence. But it isn't true. It isn't, it isn't, it isn't!'

Peter exchanged glances with Margaret. He went to his briefcase, found his address book and took it to the phone. Then hesitated, wondering where he was up to in all this, what was going on. He didn't know whether they had come and taken away the stone from the roof, or whether that door was always locked at night. Likewise, Hazel Owen might well just be shut in the offices and labs of the finishing plant waiting till morning turned a key to let her out – with whatever evidence she had gone there to find. A phone call could feasibly make things worse for her. Somebody would know to look. For a moment he stood frozen into inaction amongst so many unknowns, as his whole life seemed to be frozen just now, and at the same time rushed along willy-nilly, that perilous stillness of the wave's crest before it crashes back into an undifferentiated sea. He shivered. Then, incredibly, for no reason whatever, or like a crab scuttling sideways, called Murray.

Perhaps this was the moment of decision.

His partner's wife in Twickenham said, 'For God's sake! What time is it?'

In the hotel room Margaret and Wendy were watching. He felt he was being judged, weighed up. As by those watchful eyes in his dream. Child. Woman. Those who judge us. He hesitated, and from the open window a huge moth fluttered into the room.

But now Murray came on the line and was immediately doing the talking. 'Peter, where have you been? I was trying to get hold of you all evening, I must have called about twenty times. You're to come back tomorrow. That is, today. Okay? First plane.'

'What?'

The moth fretted audibly at the bedside lamp, slithering on the synthetic pink of the shade. Margaret hurried to close the window.

'The Australians were in touch this evening to say they've all agreed to settle out of court. You may as well come back.'

'But that's very sudden.'

'Their telex said just your being around had done the trick and to invoice them accordingly.'

Peter suddenly felt something whirring about his head.

'But I actually met Maifredi this evening and he said nothing about settling.' He flapped an arm at the thing. At the same time he remembered the constant twinkle in the fat man's eye, his inexplicable confidence.

'I was in the office at eight-thirty when it came through. It was quite clear. No point in staying on now they've decided to settle.'

Peter could think of nothing to say to this sudden adding of another dimension. Or as if the whole situation had been turned inside out. The moth was back at the lamp again, big as a bat, making shadows flit. Wendy ducked away from it.

'Apart from which, what in God's name were you calling for at this hour?'

Peter explained that the Australian woman had disappeared and the daughter had come to his door to ask for help. He had been in a quandary, since the development could prejudice their own enquiries.

'Call the police,' Murray said. 'Simple. It's not your problem.'

Peter gestured to Margaret to bring him the folder beside the bed.

'It was just that I didn't want to queer her pitch if she's gone and found some documents or something and is just having to wait till morning to get back. I thought they could be of use to us, too. I wanted to hear what you thought.'

'Yesterday maybe yes,' Murray said, 'but not now the parties have decided to settle. We're out of it now. They're not even interested in a report. They don't want to know. Oh, and by the way, Anna's been bothering me endlessly. She keeps wanting to know when you'll be back.'

So the moment had come to tell his senior partner about the fatal slab, its marked foliation and strained quartz crystals, tell-tale fragments of an incompletely absorbed country rock. Murray was an authority on such matters. He understood the danger. But again Peter hesitated. Furious, the moth fluttered dust on the top of the shade. Margaret passed him the folder.

Murray said, 'Just call the police and take the first plane home. Oh, and phone your wife before she has a nervous breakdown or gives me one.'

Still Peter hesitated. Then at last, holding the phone to his ear, looking away from the two anxious faces watching him, he realised that, rather than adding a

further problem, this development offered the unexpected solution to all the others. In the middle of the night,
these coded impulses through fibre optics had wiped out
his dilemma as if it had never been. He no longer need
choose between the honest and the dishonest report. For
no report was required of him. The fear that integrity at
work might destroy the precarious equilibrium at home
simply dissolved into thin air. All he had to do was call
the police and go. Get out. In the end he would never have
been able to leave his children anyway. His dream had
been to remind him of that. And he might yet be happy
with Anna. He wouldn't even mind another child. Then it
was the solution Margaret wanted too. He had sensed that
last night. A sudden cooling to split them apart in perfect
cleavage. She loved him. But it wasn't what she wanted
at the beginning of her adult life. Their relationship was a
burden, she had said. And he had done well to have his
fling with Thea. He had had his fun. Was ready to return.
The microfractures were only microfractures. The shear
hadn't pulled him apart. How curiously right his instinct
had been in calling Murray. The moth finally settled on
the white wall.

'Will do,' he said. 'Sorry for waking you,' and he hung
up, unable to suppress a smile. As though, lost, he had
suddenly found himself at home in his own front room.
It would be irresponsible not to call the police. The
woman was missing for God's sake. She might be hurt.
Folder in hand, he took three steps and squashed the
huge fluttering creature against the whitewash.

———— • ————

The police station floor was a cheap breccia, polygenetic
black and brown, things broken apart and then crushed
back together again. Somewhere deep beneath the earth.
The matrix must have been quite friable though, because

there were traces of an off-white filler, presumably machine-applied, on almost every tile. The flat surface is imperative. But it was fine for scraping chairs on. And obviously this bringing them here, rather than talking in the lobby of the hotel, was some sort of arrangement the police had with the management to prevent bad publicity. Annoying for him, because it might make it difficult to put a call through to Anna before the flight left. He would have to be quick as possible. Anyway, it was surely in Mrs Owen's own interest that he give as little information about her as was compatible with reporting her disappearance. Talking to a younger man dragged out of his bed because of his beginner's English, Peter explained that the woman's husband had been killed when a slab of stone fell on his head. In Australia. Unhinged, she had come here because she believed the local supplier was somehow responsible. She had left the hotel around ten o'clock the previous morning and had not returned, though she was supposed to be flying back home later today. He paused. They were worried she might have had a car accident or something. She had hired a yellow Opel.

Confabulation in the local language amidst cheap desks and filing cabinets. The police had no knowledge of an accident. Could he think of anywhere else the woman might be? Sitting by the wall and holding Wendy's hand, Margaret was eyeing him curiously, almost critically he thought.

Peter shrugged his shoulders. She just might, he said, have tried to break into the office above the finishing plant in the hope of finding some documents. She was, as he said, obsessed by the notion her husband had died due to irresponsibility on the part of the various companies involved. Then, thinking aloud, he said, 'Or I suppose she could have committed suicide.' Into the brief ensuing silence, he remarked, 'I have a flight back to London in three hours' time. My job here is finished.'

In the car going back to the hotel, Wendy turned her face to the window.

'I'll stay here with her,' Margaret whispered, 'if you'll lend me some money.'

'What?'

Night colours oxidised in the early morning. Her face was grey. The lips had lost their swollen intimacy of the evening before.

'Somebody will have to look after her. She's only seven.'

Just two hours before the flight, this particular twist had simply not occurred to him.

'But I will need some money,' she said again.

'I've only got the company credit card.' His mind hunted through the permutations. 'And if I used that it would come out. The bill itemises everything. Anyway, if you stay and the story gets into the news or something, people will know I was here with you.'

Her face had assumed a hard, smooth texture he wasn't sure he recognised. The eyes were large in the fine-grained paleness of the cheeks. The little girl still sat with her face pressed to the window. Peter was aware of being at once petty, monstrous and perfectly reasonable.

'Anyway how long would you be going to stay?' he asked.

'Oh, I imagine her mother will be back today some time.'

'But what if she isn't? What if . . .'

The big eyes narrowed sharply. The girl was right there. For heaven's sake, don't frighten her. He looked away.

Margaret whispered, 'If she really doesn't turn up, somebody will come from Australia. Meantime I'll have to stay.'

Hearing a rumbling above his head beneath clay cliffs near Sidmouth, Peter had once had to jump up and run for his life from falling boulders, only to find his bare feet painfully slowed on the tertiary shale. There had been flint, too, and he had bruised his heel badly. But these had been small considerations with the rock tumbling down behind. His feeling now was much the same: he could not be obstructed in full flight. There was too much at stake. And he snapped, 'This is ridiculous, being put in this position by that crazy woman. I have to go.'

'Peter, she didn't do it to spite you.'

He said nothing.

'Lend me some money. I'll pay it back.'

'I told you, I don't have any. I've only got the credit card.'

She said, 'Then give me the money they gave you to write the easy report.'

He turned and stared. 'Oh God, yes, I'll have to give them that back. I'd forgotten.'

'Give it to me.'

'I can't do that. It would amount to taking bribes.'

'But Peter!' He turned to find her eyes had hardened into something positively hostile. 'You've compromised yourself in every other way. I don't see why you shouldn't take their bribe. For humanitarian purposes. Anyway, I'll pay it back as soon as I can. But I'm not leaving her alone, or with the police or something. It's not right.'

'What do you mean, I've compromised myself?'

'You know something is going on and you're not the least bit interested in finding out what.'

He thought she might more reasonably have complained that the morning after asking her to live with him he was now quite desperate to get home to his wife. As though by the last escape route.

'I know nothing of the kind,' he said. 'Anyway, I've been taken off the job. The company has no more reason for paying my expenses.'

'But you told the police Hazel Owen was unhinged and obsessed, when she may very well be right. You said yourself there was something wrong with the rock.'

Wendy had turned to listen.

He said, 'They probably didn't even understand, "unhinged".'

'Peter, what's got into you?'

'What do you mean what's got into me? I've been told to go home, that's all.'

The car had arrived. He made to get out into what was now blazing early sunshine finding a sparkle in porphyry cobbles beneath the steps to the hotel. But she went on talking to his back: 'Obviously this business with their settling out of court has to do with your finding that slab and seeing it was something different. What else has happened to make them change their minds? And now you're going to let the whole thing go.'

'I'm behaving professionally,' he said.

'And I'm staying whether you leave me some money or not.'

Coming round the back of the car, she was holding the girl tightly by the hand.

'Why are you so angry?' he protested. 'I've been taken off the job. I have no choice.' He felt on edge in the fierce sunlight. England would be cooler, the lines less sharply defined, a suburban mellowness. 'I can't see any reason for attacking me,' he repeated.

'For God's sake, isn't that what you want me to do? To make things easier. You've never been like this before. But just don't do it at the expense of a little girl. All right?'

They stared at each other. And went on staring. As if their fragile relationship must snap the moment that eye contact was broken. He reached forward and embraced her. 'Margaret, Margaret! I have to go back now, you must see that.'

But then there was the phone booth.

Having whirled through the revolving doors, Margaret went to reception to ask if by chance Mrs Owen had returned. Peter slipped into the corridor and the booth to phone Anna. Her voice came on the line instantly, ringing and strong, for all its having been taken apart and put back together again. Speaking, he stared at the floor and was again struck by the boldness of the counterfeit there, an apparently red limestone that chipped grey and white, with a fossil that had never lived on each machined square. A child could have seen through it. A child. And, 'Of course you must have it,' he was saying. 'Of course.' He was only sorry they hadn't given him her faxes till just now. He'd imagined they would bring anything up to his room, and instead you had to go to a special desk and ask. 'I'm delighted you're pregnant,' he said, and felt, exactly as those words tumbled out, that he had split in two. It wasn't a question of deception. As it hadn't quite been a question of betrayal with Thea. But of layers pulling apart, the poorly-welded agglomerate of himself. He *was* pleased for her. He knew it was what she most wanted, before the child-bearing years were over. Yet he was acutely aware now, as their two voices alternated on the line, that he could not participate, physically could not. In the space left after whatever had been said, he told her she must be out of her mind talking about abortion when they had plenty of money and she so wanted the child. Crazy.

'You've been so distant,' she said. 'It's as if you'd shut yourself away from me.'

He'd tried to phone, he said. But she had been out. Then he'd been so incredibly busy.

'I meant the last year,' she said. 'The last two years. Oh Peter!'

With his toe he kicked at the biggest chip. There was no harm in a copy, so long as you didn't ask it to do the job of the original. That was the point. How could he be a father again? The kaolinite crumbled to dust. And he realised that for him the gamut of metamorphoses wasn't over yet. He hadn't arrived. He couldn't go home. Or was it just that he wanted so much to know, that that was the only aim capable of holding his personality together. He remembered how fine he had felt at his desk last night. Simply describing a slab of stone. He wanted to be back at his keyboard, powerful.

'Peter, are you there?'

'Bad line,' he explained. He asked how Sarah's play had gone.

'Great, she was great. It was a really lovely evening.'

'She wasn't upset that I wasn't there?'

'She never even mentioned it. Do you want to speak to her?'

He remembered the girl's giggles at seeing the face in the rock. Her accusations. Why? If only he could have tested the thing for shear. The evidence would have been irrefutable. And he said, 'I'll be back tomorrow evening.'

'Oh. But Murray said today. I'd been planning to sharpen the carving knife.' She laughed uncertainly.

'No room on the plane,' he said. 'There's been some kind of trade fair and everything's full. Tomorrow. I'll be back tomorrow.'

A few moments later, the lift being occupied, he was running up flight after flight of buff limestone stairs. To the roof.

———— • ————

All animals search and find. But their searching is generic. For food, for a mate, material for a nest. Or they look for something because it is theirs: lost offspring, a buried bone. Only man will search for something which is unique, but not his own, particular, but not to himself, some item he must have in the endless flux: a clue, a talisman, a precious stone. Man is infinitely more attached to the inanimate world, to the idea of dispersing and reproducing and finding himself in things: the monuments, networks, vases, tombstones. And if all of us, like lichens, are ultimately clinging to the rock, nourishing ourselves on its slow, chemical decay through the soil, only man has gone inside the rock to pull out the diamonds and the ore, to turn the earth inside out, hang granite and marble in the sky. Nothing is sacred. And his guilt and urgency, perhaps, are the fear that these things are not his own. Like slaves, they may rebel. They may not lie down in the convenient pattern, compose the required reality. Cracks may spread, questions are asked. Great panes of blue reflective glass tumble through a sub-zero morning in Massachusetts. Or stone fixings fracture in a Queensland gale. And the man prepares to defend his chequerboard, his system, his machine-made world, himself, with drawn sword. At which point, having lost what was his, or unable to find the charm that will shore up the structure, he may become dangerous, vindictive, vicious. Certainly, whoever it was had come to search Peter's room in his absence had more than lost their patience. The suitcases had been broken and emptied out on to the floor. Even the two single mattresses had been pulled from the bed. The drawers from the dresser were in an untidy pile in the middle of the room.

Margaret and Wendy stood and stared. Peter arrived with the slab in its plastic bag under his arm. The chaos in a room they had left in good order immediately generated fear and exhilaration. But in contrast to the confusion it found, Peter's mind was honed and sharpened. He walked to the computer and looked at the drive. The disk, and with it his report, was gone. The notebook which had been beside the computer likewise.

But that was not what they were after. They could have found that without making a mess.

'I've decided to stay,' he told Margaret. 'Better go down to reception and check that we can have the room for the night.'

But now the phone rang.

'Perhaps it's Mummy,' Wendy said. She was fingering her jade.

Peter picked up. It was eight forty-five a.m.

'Hello?' The voice was even and accentless. 'I thought I'd phone to say goodbye and ask if you wanted our driver to take you to the airport. I gather you have to leave.'

He hesitated.

'You see, I was planning to come along and share the back seat with you. I thought it was rather sad we were breaking off so soon.'

Even now he sensed the seduction of that voice, its curious lack of personality and consequence.

He said, 'You know perfectly well I'm travelling with my girlfriend.'

'Yes. Actually, I wanted to see what she was like. I wanted to see if there was anything that would explain your treating her so badly.'

Peter felt one more tug where he had imagined all angles and strains had already been covered. 'I can't really talk about that now,' he said.

'No, I imagine not.' And she added, 'You know, I rather like this story. Too bad we won't have time to discuss it.'

Wendy had sat down on a mattress on the floor. Margaret's face was all a question. Was there any point in asking himself whether he loved her?

Casually, he said, 'On the contrary, if I put off my flight till tomorrow, we could perfectly well meet for lunch. There are a couple of things I want to discuss, too.'

The apparent change of plan had surprised her. So he added, 'Like why somebody has just been through everything in my room. Why somebody decided to settle out of court so suddenly.'

The sound she made was somewhere between a chuckle

and a sigh. 'Peter, I think you should get on your flight.'

'Why?'

'Just get on it. Don't make this mistake.'

With his wife, he thought, she shared this wilful mysteriousness. As when Anna refused to say who some particular phone call was from. There was always some overlap somewhere. He said, 'I can't leave while I've still got that envelope to give back to you.'

'Oh don't be ridiculous.'

'It would be against my principles.'

With sudden hardness, she demanded, 'So are you going to go or aren't you?'

'No. Not yet. I want to know some more about the rock I found. Like, how much of it has been used.'

There was a short pause, a machine thinking, waiting. Then with that old tone of challenge in her voice, she said, 'If you promise to make love to me I'll pick you up in the lobby at twelve thirty.'

He was aware now of being quite lost. But that was the wrong image. How could you be lost when there was nowhere imaginable to return to? The phone call to Anna had confirmed that. Yet for all his disorientation he had never felt so alive. So able to act. Fragmented, his personality offered no constraints. 'Make it one o'clock,' he said.

Margaret asked, 'What on earth did you mention me for?'

'Just fed up of lying,' he said. 'Anyway, they can hardly think of blackmailing me if I act like I tell everybody the truth.'

Wendy asked, 'Can I have something to eat, please. I'm starving.'

———— • ————

The enigma was the only thing that offered continuity

now. Emotions and sentiment having been dispersed in all directions, there remained the excitement of the hunt, in whatever role, pursuer or pursued. This was not to say he wasn't enjoying Margaret's company hugely. Rather more so, actually, than when it had been a question of agonising over propositions. And what a useful companion she was turning out to be. It was she suggested they check out Hazel Owen's room, which, like their own, they found had been ransacked, the already packed suitcases emptied all over the floor. It was she suggested it would be a mistake to bother the management about the fact. Nothing could be achieved that way. While she re-hung Hazel Owen's clothes and Wendy picked up her dolls, Peter started to sort through the papers which had been turned upside down in the shower. There were things the Australian woman hadn't shown him: a rather shrill memorandum in which the union claimed they were being asked to work with unsafe materials; a short manual on the Use of BRG Pentaerythritol Tetranitrate in Rock Extraction; a copy of the results of the modulus of rupture tests carried out in Sydney, apparently satisfactory; two airline tickets; and, scattered here and there, like colourful accessories in a leucocratic index, a score of photographs depicting a family holiday. Presumably the last.

He gathered the photographs together to put them in their envelope and noticed how the camera was almost always in Hazel's hands, so that Jerry sometimes found it difficult to smile and show his chipped tooth, while Wendy as often as not didn't try. Standing outside a white wooden church beside her father, the girl had that reserved, withdrawn, long-suffering look some children do have, the look she was assuming now with them, as if bored by the adult world, not so much vulnerable as resigned, waiting. In fact now that she was no longer on her own in the dark the child didn't seem overly upset by her mother's absence. More irritated. She was just putting up with another of the consequences of the woman's tiresomely obsessional character: coming all this way from Australia, bothering people about her father's accident, endlessly pointing the camera to petrify happy moments. As she opened up another of her Asterix books, the slim little girl seemed so poignantly wise. She just wanted to play.

Then Peter realised that the list of figures he had in his hand must refer to the delivery schedule, how much stone had arrived when. Hazel had shown him this before, but he hadn't really looked. The page was numbered twelve and it took him another twenty minutes going through the piles of disordered papers to get back to page one and on to fifteen. An idea had occurred. And he was just beginning to get excited, though at the same time anxious, because he feared the calculations might be beyond him, when again the phone rang. The receptionist had guessed he might be in this room. The young policeman with his broken English came on the line and said the yellow Opel had now been found: on the cliffs above the sea, ten kilometres south.

When he put down the phone, Margaret asked why he hadn't told the police about the rock, about the room being searched. Peter couldn't quite answer this himself. 'They wouldn't understand,' he said. 'Too many technical details.' Whereas what he felt was that the rock was his, somehow. The enigma was his. He must unravel it. For this was the only thing that offered him a recognisable direction with an apparent goal at the end. Otherwise there was only the increasing tangle of his personal relationships, the routine he wanted and didn't want, the family matrix he hadn't the heart to smash, nor the will to subscribe to. No, if he and Margaret could spend for ever outside time, unravelling the enigma of this anomalous stone, if it kept them together just a little longer, then he might be happy. The cosmos was there for that too. And he asked the girl he loved if she was any good at using a calculator.

'Chauvinist pig,' she told him. She was expecting a first.

'If I give you all the different dimensions of the two towers and the plaza, could you work out the surface area? Bearing in mind that the main façade is in a crescent?'

They set to work. Wendy turned on the television and found Donald Duck in the local language. His own children had the video. So that as he read out the dimensions, wondering how he could approximate the window area, he again had the impression of a familiar pattern surfacing in strangeness, of being both away and at home, himself and not himself at the same time. Until, even as she laughed at Donald cubed in a meat processor, the little girl suddenly said, 'It's the stone that killed Daddy they were looking for, isn't it? That's why they searched the room.'

Peter looked up. 'Probably.'

'Is there something wrong with it?'

'Well, there's certainly something odd about it.'

'That's why you hid it?' The girl rocked backward and forward on her seat as she spoke.

'Yes.'

'Because you knew somebody else might want it.'

'I . . .'

Donald quacked ferociously.

'So what if they just walked in now? They could take it off you.'

She offered this reflection as somebody not personally interested in the affair, but willing to lend a hand. She added indifferently, 'Daddy said the rock was no good. Mummy said he was always whining and he'd get fired and we'd have nothing to eat, but then he said it was all right because they'd changed it for something better.'

'They'd changed it?'

Her eye straying back to the screen, the girl said, 'Daddy talked about work all the time. He was very boring that way.'

As his own children would get bored, Peter thought, when he pointed out that the steak on their plates contained a good ounce of pure rock material, or that the white paint they were using was actually extracted from the ilmenite in detrital black sand. They would shove a video in the machine and watch Donald endlessly killed and resurrected. Flattened by a steamroller now.

Margaret said, 'Perhaps we ought to hide it.'

Peter picked up the rock in its plastic bag and took it over to the window, as on the previous day, though there was no sun on this side of the building. He exposed a couple of inches of the stone and studied the polished side in diffuse daylight. The blood was flaking away, which was a pity. The broken edge had shed a grit of fine fragments into the plastic bag. But otherwise the slab had come through its brief fall and long journey with barely a scratch. It was tough enough not to shatter. On the other hand, when you looked at the jagged line of the breakage, there was definitely a preferred orientation to the crystals. A flow structure most probably. The microgranite of some dike or sill. But how could he take samples and test the thing if he didn't have access to their lab? Which might well not be adequate anyway. How could he say that anyone was to blame? And he knew that if he went home to do it in London, he would simply never bother. No, if he went home, it was to accept the routine, not to try to peep through this crack in it. The adventure had to do with being here, with being with Margaret, in this place which was nowhere to him.

Why had Hazel imagined he would know what to do?

'I'll be back in half an hour,' he said, 'you stay, in case someone phones.' He explained to Margaret how to use the delivery schedule and his copy of the tender specifications to work out the surface area of stone actually delivered. Then she should take into account the percentage of rejects as described in the telex he'd read her the other morning – which was, where, here – and so calculate what floor, give or take one or two, they ought to have been at in mid-May when the slab he now held tucked under his arm had split off from its spandrel panel and fallen. They had said the twentieth. 'Got it?'

She saw at once what his idea was, and smiled him a decidedly new smile, a sort of busy, intelligent complicity. Anna would not have been capable. Anna would have become hysterical. But then Anna was an excellent mother, sang a sweet counterpoint alto at St Barnabas: Handel, Bach, Ancient & Modern. So that getting into the lift, he wondered if it wasn't just a question of keeping everything in its right compartment, or discreetly deployed along the right surface of oneself. Always touching you, but never meeting. The way atoms knew to cluster, and then crystals. It was when nature's compartments began to break down that everything precipitated. Though that, too, was nature. When you raised the temperature, usually.

Peter shook his head. Never had thoughts raced so fast and so unpredictably. He felt drunk with the excitement of it all. Which was also a kind of self-destruction. In the lobby he stopped to wonder if the person who had searched their rooms mightn't be waiting there to accost him. A small group of orientals were huddled round the revolving doors, taking up about a dozen of the floor's syenite slabs. Not an attractive choice.

Then the receptionist called him to the desk. She had London on the line. The booth was occupied, so he took the call right there on the counter of microfractured grey pearl with the young woman's cigarette smoke drifting into his eyes. Her short helmet of hair seemed part of the uniform. She was smiling, watching. And her smiling seemed part of the uniform too.

Murray said, 'I hear you're not back till tomorrow now, what's up?'

Instinctively Peter said, 'For heaven's sake, how come you talk to Anna so often?'

'It's not my fault if she phones me. She was concerned because I had told her you would be coming back today.'

'I can't see why she's worried. I gave her a perfectly good excuse.'

'Ah, so it was an excuse.'

'Look, this Australian woman's gone missing. I don't know. Her daughter's only seven and she's entirely on her own. I wanted to make sure there was somebody to look after her.'

'And I want you back here as soon as possible.'

'Tomorrow's Saturday,' Peter said. 'I've hardly slept. I can't see what the hurry is. I'll pay any extra expense myself, if that's the problem. Today I'll just rest.'

There was a pause. A faint ratchetting sound disturbed the line. Or as though springs were ticking as they slowly soaked up strain. The receptionist smiled. In its plastic bag the fatal slab was weighing on his arm. Sweating slightly, Peter said, 'Murray, listen, you don't happen to know more about this situation here than you're letting on, do you? You know I found . . .'

'Just come back,' the senior partner said, clearly irritated. 'The authorities will look after the girl. We're not a charity.'

'Just tell me,' Peter said, 'which of the companies it was asked to settle? Because . . .'

Murray actually laughed, and this was rare. Likewise the use of his junior partner's name which followed, 'Peter, don't be an ass. Your wife's waiting for you. There's an urgent quarry feasibility job Monday morning. A couple of days in Derbyshire. You can take your young lady there, if that's what you're worried about.'

'What young lady?' But apparently another compartment had gone. His hand resting on the polished granite shook.

'Oh come on, Peter. Everybody knows. You've been going about like a fart in a trance for the last three months. One could hardly say you've been discreet. Why do you think your wife's gone so completely off her rocker? Now be sensible, get on the plane and I'll see you with this brief first thing Monday morning.'

———— • ————

When you stopped your ears to the modern background noise, when you looked aside from the perfect right angles, the lines of parked cars, the compelling neon through plate glass, then the fossil structure that was the lost culture of these islands emerged quite plainly. They had been the centre of the world then, producing the vases and statues that would assert their stories, creating the moulds that would allow an artefact to be copied time after time, the written word that could reproduce anything. Or nothing. Turning at random through an open gate, trying to see whether he was really being followed or whether it was just creeping paranoia, Peter found himself walking amongst the stumps and stones of what must once have been a small temple, now enclosed in the forecourt of some government building.

He stood and read a plaque, all the time glancing over one shoulder. A group of diligent tourists were transposing the old geometry into the new through the lenses of their cameras. It was a mere 2500 years ago and broken fragments of a frieze arranged on a display case under dirty glass showed two robed female figures. In four languages a plaque said, 'Identical Nemeses, guardians of the cosmic law. One holds a set square, the other the urn where lots are cast.' Peter stared. The stone, he noted, was a fine-grained limestone, severely weathered. As well it might be.

Walking on down the broad street that led to the sea, he reflected that this was the fifth day he had been on the island and the weather had never changed. Always this too-dazzling blue, and the fierce sun you knew was there but could never look at. It was at once perfect and oppressive. As though the light that so neatly scissored and pasted the parking-meters, palms and stuccoed façades, had somehow cut him off from his past life or any imaginable future. He was frozen here in the high noon of an anodyne sensuality. Holiday weather.

While back at home they all knew.

He crossed the road that ran along the sea-front and descended three steps to the beach. Almost immediately the irritated surge of the traffic chafing in its well-marked boundaries gave way to shriller human cries, laughter and chatter across the hot white sand between the sunshades. And it was impossible, for all the urgent situation, not to notice the girls. What obsession it must have taken to copy those curves in stone, the postures of torso and thigh. Identical Nemeses indeed! Why did there have to be two of them? And why did he suddenly feel there was no real hurry, despite the way events were precipitating?

The sea was motionless. He moved along the rows until he found the coordinates of the sunshade they had rented, five down twenty-two along. Two deckchairs leaned against a cement base. He opened one out, sat, placed the plastic bag with its stone beneath his feet, and, while children played all around, fathers smoked, mothers read papers or went off to swim, he slowly worked the igneous rock down into this quartz sand. He thought he would have liked to have been a tourist, to have let his body be drenched in sunlight, to have photographed the ruins. But he had never done that kind of thing, never moved easily between work and play. Rather he was always collecting, finding the grains and crystals in the rocks, seeing the downward creep of the landscape in the curve of a tree-trunk, guessing at the bedrock from the soil it bred. Anna complained: he didn't do things when things needed doing; he didn't relax when it was time to relax. But he found his observations reassuring. Beyond any religious or social vision. Perhaps even beyond his love for Margaret. Who had both jolted him out of his reveries and started the whole process off all over again. The way he was always seeing her in terms of this compound or that, this texture, this colour, this beauty.

Margaret. His pearl.

Peter worked the offending rock down into the sand. It was well covered now, perhaps two or three inches down. No one would dream of looking here. Then he was just standing to leave, when he saw Mrs Owen.

It was a fleeting glimpse through the kaleidoscope of sunshades and bathing costumes, the heat shimmer above the sand. She was in black again, a blemish, a wedge of shadow in the painful colour and light. Peter started to move. Then a tall negro was in his way, offering a tray of trinkets. He had lost her. There were so many people. He was wearing office shirt and trousers, his big, Clark's shoes sinking in the sand. Sweating. She had been down by the sea. Perhaps even paddling in it. The soft sand absorbed his attempts to run. Everybody else was moving so slowly, so aimlessly. So that as though in a dream he seemed semi-paralysed, everything obstructed him. He stumbled down the aisle between the sunshades, avoided a flying tennis ball, a child's sandcastle. Then when he saw her again, quite some distance away, at the water's edge, he called her name. 'Hazel. Hazel!' She was with someone. She was walking beside a tall man in blue shorts. 'Hazel!' His voice was lost in the cries of the beach. No one so much as turned. 'Hazel!' She was in the thickest of the crowd at the water's edge, moving slow and upright through the joggers and bathers, the fatties filling their lungs with iodine, the mothers sitting with their toddlers in the shallows. Still fifty yards away. He ran round a sail boat they were dragging up the sand, then past the lifeguard's look-out chair. To the left was the great, flat shimmer of the sea, drawn to distinction only by the cone of the volcano. Then the wheeling sky, the birds, the highrise lattice of the sea-front hotels, the angular old hills behind. He had lost her again.

He stopped, breathless, debilitated by this heat which seemed to demand he change in some way, adapt. He scanned the patch of water and sand where she must be. She must. He had recognised the walk, the hair. Or something. Whatever it was you did recognise about people. A presence. Their uniqueness, presumably. Though why she was down here on the beach he couldn't imagine. She had arranged to meet somebody, perhaps. Somebody from the company who had agreed to tell her something. 'Hazel!' There she was again. Further off than he had expected. Barefoot in the sea, it seemed. A woman in a black dress, a man in blue shorts, a white T-shirt. 'Hazel!'

But there was the drone of an engine now. A hum rapidly became a roar. Children screamed and waved, splashing water on his shoes and trouser bottoms as he ran along where the brine frothed on the sand's edge. Flying low, in perfect parallel to the beach, a small plane appeared. But he would catch up with her now, even if his voice was drowned out. He couldn't lose her now.

The plane raced by, towing an advertisement for a soda drink, a huge, long rectangle of some orange plastic fabric pulled tight by wind and speed. It drew a knife-straight line along the shore, as though to sever sea from land. But he could recognise the handbag she had rummaged in now. The beach sloped shallowly, so that five or six yards out the water was only up to her ankles. Peter was shouting himself hoarse, but she wouldn't hear him. She had the same simple black dress she had had on that morning over the breakfast which had marked the beginning of the end of his idyll with Margaret. And she and the taller man beside her moved slowly through the water, their backs towards him, the man's arm round her waist, a dark tattoo just below the shoulder.

Peter splashed out after them despite shoes and trousers.

'Hazel, what in God's name are you doing here?'

He froze a yard or so behind them. They too had stopped. Staring out to sea. To the volcano. The man's arm was round her waist, pulling her slightly towards him. She was running light fingers on the white skin inside his elbow. Her body was leant against him. Yet Hazel Owen had said her dead husband was so precious. That there could never be another Jerry in her life, only the pursuit of those who had so carelessly sacrificed him to the wheels of their machine. He stared at the two enigmatic figures. Something about them. Her head had come to rest on his shoulder. Beside the dark tattoo. There was a pink ribbon round her neck he hadn't seen her wear before and a strip of seaweed clung to her calf just below the black hem of her dress. They straightened and made as if to turn.

Peter fled, splashing through the water to the shore. Without looking back, he raced across the sand. It no longer seemed to slow his progress, rather to urge him on. And the sun had suddenly lifted its weight too. The air was cool, breatheable, even cold. At the first bar along the waterfront he had a double brandy with ice and examined a marble table-top with a fine tracery of magnetite impurities.

———— ● ————

Fifteen minutes later, as he pushed through the revolving

doors of the hotel, Peter found Margaret hanging on the phone at reception, waiting impatiently for someone to come on the line. Clearly upset, she fished in a pocket and handed him a crumpled piece of paper. The note was written in an endearingly childish script, round and unformed as infant faces are.

'I was taking a shower,' Margaret explained.

Wendy had written, 'I'm going to find Mum and make her take me home. I don't see why you should worry about her. She's disappeared before. You've been very kind. WENDY.'

Margaret had been searching the surrounding streets for almost an hour. He watched her urgent expression as she spoke, aware again of how young she was, and sensible. After she had finally got her connection and told the police, they went up to their room to wait for them to arrive. In the corridor a woman was moving a polishing machine in slow curves over the floor. The air had a closed, waxy, mausoleum smell. Under their door in an open envelope was a fax, scribbled: 'Peter, I just wanted to tell you how glad I am. It was so nice to hear your voice. I'll be at the airport tomorrow. There's only one flight, isn't there? Forgive me for being my normal hysterical self. All my love. ANNA. 'Ps. Don't forget presents for the kids!'

Peter went to the phone and dialled the number of the finishing plant. A brusque voice came on to the line. He asked to speak to the manager. The voice was incomprehensible. But he couldn't remember the manager's name. 'The manager,' he repeated. 'Anybody who speaks English.' The voice talked for perhaps thirty seconds. The tone was recognisably impatient, but the message obscure. He waited for a moment. Again the voice said something, again incomprehensible. He hung up.

'You should have told the police to go there right away. She might have taken a cab.'

'I don't think she had any money.'

They sat in the room, Margaret on the now re-made bed, he at the desk by the computer from which his report had been stolen. She put her head in her hands and there was a long silence between them.

'This is awful,' she said at last.

'Margaret,' he said.

She looked up, still shaking her head. 'I don't know why, but I feel guilty.'

He found her eyes and waited. There was something different between them. A new but bitterer well of intimacy had been tapped.

'I just keep thinking of this woman, and of Anna, too. I feel responsible. I mean, I've just been here having a holiday while they . . .' She sighed, shook her head. But now she looked up and smiled. 'Peter.' She liked to say his name. 'It's odd when we're together and not making love, isn't it?'

He let a few seconds pass, sitting in the drab room, all impetus lost with this new complication. They could do nothing till the police came. Then he told her, 'It's been the best part of my life, these last months. Like finding a vein I didn't even know was there.'

'Vein, as in rich ore deposit, of course?' she smiled.

'As in gemstone,' he laughed, 'but warm with blood, too.'

There had always been so much wondering eye contact between them. Now it became a sort of wistful mingling in each other. As if everything was decided, over – she had made that so clear – and yet everything still to play for. Merely because they were still there looking at each other.

'Bloodstone, if you like,' he said.

'Is there such a thing?'

He sighed. 'Chalcedony flecked with red jasper. One of the silica group.' Then he added, 'Just another rock in the end, love.'

They were both silent. There was the hum of traffic outside, fretting in its stone straitjacket.

'Just another rock,' he repeated.

She said very sensibly, 'We should never have come, Peter. We shouldn't have mixed ourselves up with all this. We were all right on our own. We had our world. This has spoilt everything.'

'I'd like to make love,' he said.

Again she smiled. 'I just can't help thinking, if I hadn't come, you know, maybe none of this would have happened. As though our affair caused it somehow. On your own, you would have sorted the whole situation out right from the start.'

'If you hadn't been here I would just have gone home when I was told to. There would have been no "situation".'

As they looked at each other he was aware of so much affection. He should never have gone to bed with Thea. Unless it was precisely that shattering of their complicity which had now brought them together in this different way, searching for each other again.

'Assuming we fly back tomorrow,' he said, determinedly. 'What if I come and live with you immediately?'

She was silent.

'Murray phoned when I was down in the lobby. Apparently everybody knows about us.'

She didn't say anything at all. But again her great brown eyes were holding his.

'He said the way I'd been acting it was obvious.'

'Even Anna?' she asked.

'He implied that. He said they were all just waiting for me to "get over it".'

She frowned hard. 'Still she seems determined for you to come back. You must have said something very nice to her on the phone this morning.'

He pulled a face.

'She must care a great deal for you.'

'Yes.'

But he knew this was instinct, the children, the way everybody felt so responsible for their immaturity, for that lack of definition they had. As if we parents were the only makers. We had to form the perfect mould and wait for them to set into it. When quite probably it was as much a question of time and cooling as anything else.

He said, 'I suppose it should even be reassuring. But what I wanted was what I had with you.' They both noticed the past tense. Which would have been unthinkable only a couple of days before. 'I thought we were going to arrive at something miraculous.'

'Peter.'

They stared at each other. Very slowly she was shaking her head.

'Anyway, what Murray was trying to say on the phone was that I was only staying on here to prolong things with you and I should come home at once.'

'And are you?'

'I didn't think so when I decided. I thought I wanted to get to the bottom of what's going on. But perhaps he's right. Perhaps it's just a matter of not wanting to let go, or not wanting to go home. Hence my invitation. Which is serious. Not just a fantasy.'

Saying this he contrived to feel at once terribly sure of himself, quite desperate and hopelessly resigned.

'So I say yes and we go back and live happily ever after, while Anna keeps the children?'

'Well . . .' It did seem improbable when she put it so brutally, the unlikely hypothesis behind some expensive experiment only government funds could afford to sponsor. But the vision was there. And he said, 'Yes. Why not?'

'No,' she said.

The phone rang. The police were in reception.

Going down in the lift, she said, 'By the way, they should have been on the fifteenth floor. Not the twentieth.'

'What?'

'The cladding. I worked it out. Give or take a floor or two, depending on the window area, they should have been on the fifteenth.'

———— • ————

There are elements that change so completely they appear to have disappeared. They are hidden in a compound now, or have escaped into the atmosphere. No end of ingenuity will suffice to retrieve them. And yet one tries. Peter and Margaret described Wendy to the police, gave the two men some photos, reminded the one with the elementary English that he had seen the girl himself earlier this morning, explained that she had changed into a white blouse and pink skirt. As much individuality as they could muster. Though now she wasn't there, it was already difficult to remember exactly how tall she was, how slim or otherwise. Either people were there or they weren't. Obviously, if the police had to look for her amongst the milling thousands on the beach it would be hopeless. But if she had started to walk into the hills to where she imagined the car had been found on the cliffs, then the dark tarred road, the empty landscape, the pink skirt would betray her.

'I decided I'd better not leave till tomorrow,' Peter was saying, when a hand took his elbow and a voice said, 'I believe we have an appointment.' Thea.

There were the two young policemen, then Margaret and himself, standing where the receptionist had ushered them to one unobtrusive corner of the lobby. The two women exchanged mere glances.

'I'm supposed to see Dr Maifredi for lunch,' Peter invented for Margaret. 'Can you hold the fort? Two hours?' In a whisper he added, 'I'm going to wring something out of them.'

Thea was smiling. She wore a light-coloured tailleur, her jet-black hair pinned above her head with a simple white clip, to then flow down over her shoulders. Margaret hardly seemed to notice. She was rummaging through pockets for the note the girl had left, explaining when it had happened, the streets she herself had immediately searched. Only the younger of the two policemen raised an eyebrow: 'Dr Maifredi?' he said respectfully, and nodded politely to Thea.

In the car, Peter said brusquely, 'Look, tell me right away, do you know where they are?'

'The girl's missing now too, is she?'

'Yes. For the last couple of hours.'

There was a studied pause while Thea went through the motions of starting the car. They circled the small statue and accelerated into one of the wider streets.

'Why would I know where they are?'

So, despite what he felt were the dramatically changed circumstances, she was offering only the laconic back and forth of their previous conversations. Irritated, he said, 'Because Hazel Owen knew the rock was different, and she was determined to find out why. Probably she went to the finishing plant to see if she could steal some documents. Or to one of those other quarries the company has, to see what was being brought up. And maybe it has something to do with somebody's deciding to settle out of court the very same day.'

Under the dazzle of the midday sun, a heat shimmer rose from the asphalt. Thea braked, pulled the car over to the side, stopped, then was silent for a moment. Looking straight ahead through the glare of the windscreen, her profile might have been cut out of a magazine, detached. He could see the clean line of her breasts. Without the air moving through the windows the heat was suddenly palpable and oppressive.

With habitual irony, she asked, 'Now, are we going

to make love, or not?'

Peter said, 'I'd like to settle this other thing first.'

She turned to him. 'Do you really care what happened to this man, Jerry Owen?'

He said, 'Yes.' But too automatically. Her perfume was already exciting him, reminding him of their embraces.

'Why? You never met the man. You didn't know him.'

Peter cast about. When he thought of Jerry Owen it was always the chipped tooth that came to mind. The one feature they shared in common. He said, 'I'm interested.'

'You're interested. Why?'

'He was a person, alive, now he's dead. It's a big change.'

'He and a few million others every day.'

'He was killed by a rock. I'm an expert on rock.'

'But he wasn't exactly stoned to death. It was an accident.'

Peter said, 'It's a question of proximity. I've become involved. I got to know Mrs Owen a bit and her daughter. People become special. I like them. I said I'd help.'

'But help in what way? You surprise me. I thought you were more intelligent.'

'Help to see if anybody was criminally responsible. The woman was desperate to know.'

Thea said, 'Mrs Owen is a lost case. Of what possible use can it be for her to keep worrying about him? He wasn't murdered. She should be thinking of her child. She should get herself another husband. What's the point of attaching yourself to one person like that, as if we weren't separate people with separate lives. He's dead.'

Peter felt all the power of this argument. 'She loved him,' he said.

Thea burst out laughing. 'And do you love your little girlfriend?' Not waiting for an answer, she started the car again and pulled away rapidly. But then took the opportunity of a filling station to turn round.

'Where are we going?'

'To my father's house.'

'So we're not going to make love?' He felt the inevitable combination of relief and disappointment. And was immediately hankering for the guilt and excitement of a moment before. There was a terrible reactivity about these two compounds, the way they resisted all attempts at separation, or some more convenient combination.

'Do you want to make love?' she asked.

'Do you?'

She said, yes.

'Why?'

'Because I like it. I like you.'

'Despite my little girl.'

She laughed again, as one who is always viewing the situation from higher up, further off. 'Maybe because of her. Why should I be worried about your having a girlfriend? On the contrary, it excites me. She looks very nice. We can imagine she's watching us if you like.'

Peter flinched. 'But don't you ever want to have a . . . a relationship? Something permanent? No, okay, okay, I know there's nothing permanent. I mean, don't you want to share something special with someone, to know that they're attached to you in a special way?'

She said coolly, 'I have a relationship with my father. It's all I need.' She added, 'If we feel like it we can make love there. He'll have his siesta. I like to swim after sex.' She turned to him for a moment from her driving. Her voice had a sudden honesty. 'I've never heard anyone explain why one shouldn't enjoy oneself if one wants to. I actually like you, Peter. I was sorry when I heard you were leaving.'

'But I don't understand why we have to go to your father's.'

Laughing now she said, 'Because he told me that if you decided to stay then I should bring you to him.'

'So when you called, it was to find out if I was leaving and to bring me to your father if I wasn't.'

She shrugged her shoulders.

They were silent. There was the steep, twisting climb into the hills, the cypresses at every bend, the glow of dry light on brightly mottled scrub, the etched rigidity of a prehistoric tower, testimony to a first groping for that more coercive geometry that triumphed now in a line of giant pylons marching up from the coast. He said, 'At one point it occurred to me you might be planning to blackmail me. To have me write a decent report. I mean, by having sex with me.'

'Bit of that,' she laughed.

He trod as though barefoot over flint. 'And your father knew?'

'Of course. We have no secrets.'

'You were told to seduce me?'

'I do what I like,' she replied lightly.

He said, 'You see how much you can't know about people just by looking at them.'

Inevitably there was the tinkle of laughter. Its small assertion of superiority. Or as if she were always claiming the right to be the one who coloured the conversation, gave it its mood and texture.

'There are ways and ways of knowing,' she said. 'I think you knew perfectly well, actually. It was that that excited you.' With wry candour she added, 'My father likes me to have plenty of men for two reasons. First, I think he fantasises about it. Second, it means I'm less likely to marry. He likes those myths where there are lots of suitors but none of them can ever marry the girl. Then of course, if an affair is useful for work too, all the better.' She paused. 'We will tell your little girlfriend about it if you don't agree to what we have in mind. You understand that, don't you? And your wife.'

Immediately after making this threat, she laid her free

hand on his leg. There were the slim fingers, the gold and the diamond, her perfume and low voice. Confusion became exquisite. While beneath that confusion he once again had the impression of being under some kind of exemplary strain, the object of a destructive experiment, where they were just waiting for the test piece to shatter so they could measure the load applied, check the temperature, the pressure, and say, Yes, that was it, that's what we can expect from others like him.

'Men are funny,' she laughed. 'The fact that you betrayed her shows you've just made another wife of her. Men always have to have a woman to betray and another to betray them with. Somehow I always manage to be the latter.'

He couldn't answer her. But he felt the pain of it. She made him banal. And Margaret had said no.

'Probably,' she said, as though these things were common knowledge, 'betraying your wife didn't mean anything any more because you've stopped having sex with her.'

He felt he should object to this. She reduced him to the passivity of a rock beneath hammer blows. When he should have been thinking about the missing woman, her daughter.

She said softly, 'I'm going to fuck you and fuck you now. I'm going to make you feel good and guilty, so you know you're alive. Then you will talk to my father and we will sort this stupid business out and you can go home.'

Involuntarily, Peter said, 'With you it's pure sex, just life. But with Margaret, it's Margaret.'

Immediately he realised that this was the key. He had said something important. And in fact she jerked on the brakes. The car had been racing along a straight stretch of road that followed a high ridge. There was the ever-hazy sea away to their left, the well-defined pattern of hill and valley to the right, slashed by roads and punctuated by villages, villas, towers, pylons. The car slewed to a stop by a stone wall. Her hand tightened on his thigh. 'Just life!' She shook her head, lips pouting in a mocking smile. 'Just life, just death, no?' She laughed immoderately as though for once not quite in control of herself and pulled out on to the road again.

Five minutes later, at the automatic gate, she asked, 'Do you know the story of Oenomaus and Hippodameia?'

He didn't answer.

'He was her father. A king. He killed her suitors and hung their heads outside the palace gate. My father has a vase.'

'Until somebody killed him, presumably,' Peter said. Then with a surge of decision, quite unpremeditated, or perhaps because he felt deeply humiliated by everything that had passed between them, he said, 'I only want to see your father. I'm not interested in making love.'

Quite cheerfully, she said, 'What a fool you are.' And she was so strikingly beautiful, getting out of the car, walking across raked white aggregate, so much the perfect specimen, that he already felt a pang of regret.

Day Five

Afternoon

The first hominid fossils appear in the Pliocene of the Tertiary. How long would it be before man learnt to copy the hostile nature he found all about him, sketch buffalo and spear on walls of rock? Until shortly before history began. But nature was already a masterful counterfeiter of herself: twinned aragonite will often appear to be single crystals of a higher symmetry. Spring snow on dark branches can seem miles of cherry blossom along the foothills of the Alps. And any frog knows how to look like tree bark or waterweed. When man discovered camouflage, he was only copying nature copying herself. And from then on, as if in a hall of mirrors the copies proliferated. Perhaps that's what history is: idols, images, stone dogs guarding Egyptian tombs, household objects, behaviour patterns, institutions, shapes. Until everything begins to fall in with an underlying pattern, a denser and denser mesh. Which might be necessity. Certainly the copies ripple ever outwards now – there's no reversing the process – carried along wires, through the air, rotated on fluorescent screens. A prodigious marshalling. Sitting on Maifredi's high terrace, Peter was struck by the way every surface, shape, tile, seemed to reflect or reproduce another. It began with the strong pink rectangle of the house and then spread across the square terrace with its granite chequer; below that there was the pool, a parallelogram of lawn with sprinkler system, the trim ranks of the flowerbeds, some carefully stepped landscaping reflected in the lacquer of polished cars, and then again the trained fruit trees, their branches at right angles, the crushed limestone of the drive in its neat porphyry margins, and so on and on as far as the perimeter wall and the oppressive verticality of its railings serrating the horizon.

He might never have noticed it had he not been in a strange place. But here it was unmistakeable. Some central principal had been isolated, perfected and then reproduced time after time in stupefying succession, dazzling almost, the way gridwork on a page can dazzle the eye. So that nothing was quite itself and nothing but. But always part. As he himself could never quite decide who he might be outside those relationships he had copied from everybody else, the people on each side of him: marriage, work, parenthood. And when you fled for identity outside that framework, it was only to confirm the prison. Everybody had a mistress. Their view from a window. Everybody had a further wilder adventure to dip their toes in the void beyond, to hear someone say with a hollow laugh: 'just life, just death'. Then drew their foot in fast. So that if one of the heavy rectangular shutters directly above were to fall on him now, if one of the square terracotta roof-tiles were to slither across copper guttering over his head to crash down and split his skull, Peter wasn't exactly sure who it was such culprits would be killing.

Moving to the edge of the parapet, he looked down into the pool. Thea swam back and forth in a chemical blue element that copied the sea reflecting the sky. She was naked today. Two black lines had been painted on the cement to stop her from wandering from the perpendicular. At each end she did a neat tumbleturn, each the exact replica of the one before. Peter stared at the smooth, slow movement of her flanks and thighs, a goddess at her bath, then turned as the Asian maid came out on the terrace to beckon him in.

Maifredi was eating. The big table was antique in

the modern open-plan that led through from terrace to staircase. Another man sat to one side of him to make a corner. The wife was knitting by the window, just as she had been two days ago. Or was it three? The regular click of the needles seemed unnaturally loud, imposing its rhythm. There were vases lined up in their stillness. Then the maid ushered him to a third place laid at table, opposite the stranger.

'Welcome!' Maifredi was predictably hearty. 'I must present to you Mr Dick Frye. He works for your client. He arrived yesterday in the evening.'

They were eating what might have been pigeons. Two or three small corpses on each plate. Now the maid was bringing another for him. Maifredi had his mouth full as he spoke. Frye was stiffer and more formal: tall, nordic blond, a bony seriousness about him. Maifredi invited Peter to turn over his glass and poured out a crimson wine. Above the table and Frye's head, and thus opposite the new arrival, a framed black-and-white photograph some eight feet long reproduced what must be a temple frieze. He hadn't noticed it on his first visit. And it was striking how fluid the gestures of horse and warrior seemed in the prison of their stone patterning, flattened now in silver phosphate. 'Cheers,' Maifredi said. 'Eat first, then we'll talk.'

Peter was aware of a carefully orchestrated coercion, the constant thwarting of his sense of urgency. Yet he felt unable to resist it, as if forced to wait for his small part in this complex choreographed whole. On his plate, the tiny birds were dark grey in colour, and Maifredi was explaining to both guests how one took their Malteser-sized heads between one's teeth, crushed and sucked. That was the best part. He had a vase showing them being caught in nets some two thousand and more years before, a tradition still practised on the island, albeit illegally. There was something dreadfully embryonic about the creatures, Peter thought, reminding him of fallen fledglings on spring pavements. Though the taste was exquisite. Drinking from his wine, he said determinedly, 'Somebody searched my room this morning.'

Maifredi chewed, allowing a small trickle of something to escape on his chin. Frye was stony faced. Maifredi used his napkin and laughed. 'I have told you our geologist is extraordinary.'

Frye said quickly, 'Presumably your company has been in touch to let you know that we consider your brief closed. As of yesterday. The whole matter is being settled out of court. You have been extremely useful and we are grateful.' His voice was polite, but firm.

Peter said, 'That doesn't really explain the fact that somebody searched my room.'

There was loud laughter. Like his daughter, Maifredi used mirth as a means of intimidation. 'You know,' he chuckled, 'I imagined when I hear you are staying that you just want to – what is that fine word the Americans use – pork your lovely little girl for a couple of days. And instead no! You are still worrying about this boring stone!'

Peter said evenly, 'Presumably somebody else was worried about it if they felt they needed to search my room. I'd like to know why.'

Maifredi grunted, shook his head, and proceeded to clear his plate. But Frye said stiffly, 'That slab is actually the property of the Marlborough Place Project.'

'Oh come come!' Their fat host allowed droplets to splutter from his lips. 'Come, come.' Very quickly he picked up his glass and drained it. 'Why do we argue? We are all in the same business. I insist we finish to eat before discussing this. It is not polite.'

His mind racing, Peter ate automatically. He felt strength surge when he used it, but at the same time it scared him. Clearly it would be wiser to be on the plane home. Or at least enjoying Margaret's company while he could. The only urgent matter was the missing woman and her daughter, and he saw no part he could play there. No doubt the police would find them soon enough, wandering about the island. Perhaps if he just asked for assurances that no more slabs would fall, that was all that could reasonably be asked of him. Some explanation of the technical measures they had no doubt taken. A show of responsibility. They couldn't be that foolhardy.

Frye ate slowly, without relish. The bony face might have been carved from some rugged Australian outcrop. Meanwhile, the even clicking of the wife's needles in her armchair surfaced in this gap in the conversation, and became irritating now, meshing the silence into a web of monotonous resignation. What could she be knitting in this heat? Why wasn't she at table, playing hostess? Looking up at the big vase on the shelf behind Maifredi, Peter asked suddenly, 'Why does the woman have those ribbons hanging from her?'

Maifredi looked round, as if glad to have the chance, cheered by the change of subject. His whole fat body shifted on the chair, flesh gathering and stretching. Some three feet high, the vase showed, red on white, a group of robed figures grouped around an altar. 'It's a marriage,' he said, still eating. 'The ribbon she wears is representing the, what do you say, the veil? Yes, the veil that separates . . .'

Thea had come into the room through open terrace windows. He raised his voice and spoke to her in their own language. It was curious how a voice could retain the same tones and suddenly become opaque, incomprehensible. Wearing a red bathrobe, hair glistening wet, she stepped up to the table. 'The veil? It separates the sacred and the profane. Our world from the other. Actually they were tassles of wool and people hung them on brides, and on animals to be sacrificed too, or on your bed if you were dying.'

Maifredi spoke again. Thea added, 'Athletes were given them when they won their races. They bound them round their knees and ankles.'

But the fat man still wasn't happy. The subject excited him. 'It is more complicated, Mr Nicholson. The veil signifies also the excess in life, when you become touched by the other, that is by a god. You lose control. Everything that is more than just the, well, the routine.'

Frye had finished eating and sat up, poker-faced. Peter was staring at the graceful figures, detached from the background, but flowing together in a harmonious group round their ceremony.

'Perhaps if you come often you will take an interest,' Maifredi said warmly. 'I begin to like you, Mr Nicholson. It needs a good eye to see such details as the ribbons. I mean, they are always there in the vases and friezes, but nobody is seeing them.' His smile seemed genuine. 'The offer I make on the boat is a real offer. You come here when you like. Bring your girlfriend.'

Standing behind him, massaging the fat shoulders, Thea winked.

Peter said, 'I saw Mrs Owen this morning. She had a ribbon tied around her neck.'

Their silence was complete. The clicking of the needles immediately became audible again. Frye turned to quiz Maifredi who for the first time seemed to have lost his sense of humour. His eyes shrank into the fat cheeks.

'I beg your pardon, Mr Nicholson, but . . .'

'I saw Mrs Owen. She had a ribbon hanging from her neck. Pink.'

There was a further silence. Thea was staring at him, while her fingers pressed hard into her father's shoulders.

'You don't say,' Frye said at last. 'Good.' But his eyes on Peter's face were shrewd.

Peter hesitated. 'It was on the beach. I didn't manage to talk to her. She was with a man.' He remembered the combination of heat and glare, the plane with its Fanta ad. 'I only saw her from behind.'

With a condescending smile, Frye said, 'Then maybe it wasn't her.' It was odd that he should share the woman's Australian accent.

Peter said, 'I don't usually have any problems recognising people.'

Thea's hands were still kneading her father's shoulders. His face had lost all its blood, the jowls apparently drained to chalk. 'A ribbon?' he said softly. But she bent down and whispered to him. Her cheek seemed to be almost caressing his. Frye looked from Maifredi to Peter and back again. Thea said, 'My father would like to retire to his room for his siesta. We can discuss the matter later.'

'No,' Peter said determinedly. 'No, I only need to ask a few questions. There's no point in waiting.' He paused, surprised to find one could impose oneself so easily. The tension was palpable. The knitting needles beat their rhythm, jerking the wool back and forth. 'I just want to know why your two companies agreed to settle out of court.'

'That's plainly none of your business,' Frye snapped. 'As I see it, there is nothing to discuss. You return the stone to us and get out of here.'

Enunciating slowly, Peter said, 'There are at least five floors of those same slabs already on the façade, I don't see why you should be so worried about this particular one.'

Frye sat up and stared. He turned to Maifredi for help. Still pale, the fat man again spoke to Thea in their own language. She went over to a cabinet, returning with a bottle. The Asian maid, who had been hovering, went off, presumably to get some glasses.

Thea asked, 'Would you like some sweet? We can have a trolley brought in.'

'I assume,' Peter said, 'that the number of stones rejected by the workers was making it impossible to keep things to schedule, with the prospect of considerable losses for the proprietor and fines for the contractor. At which point somebody, contractor or proprietor, went to an alternative supplier and got a different rock, more suitable for engineering to these tolerances, free from the microfractures that were bothering the unions, but not in fact as resistant to shear. Presumably, awareness of this after I brought that slab to the quarry yesterday is what has allowed you, Dr Maifredi, to convince our mutual client in the space of just a few hours to settle your differences out of court, or perhaps let the matter drop entirely. All the same, whoever chose to accept that stone may well be criminally responsible for Mr Owen's death. It is a microgranite with an evident flow structure and marked foliation. It can't have anything like the same mechanical qualities required in the original tender for the stone, not to mention the further qualities required after the new fixing method was adopted.'

As on the previous evening when he had written it down in such a hurry on his computer, Peter experienced the sense of power that comes from understanding, a splendid feeling of direction and well-being. However dangerous this might be.

Frye had the fingers of big, square hands twined together over the tablecloth and was tightening and releasing them. Maifredi drank a brandy with one tip of his glass, pushed back his chair from the table, unbuckled the belt of his white trousers and sighed. 'This is all correct,' he said. 'Oh dear.' He took a small cigar and threw the pack on to the table. 'It is also correct that Mr Frye is gone to your room this morning to remove the stone.'

The other man turned, apparently to protest.

'Not to worry, Mr Frye. Not to worry. The important thing we must know, is what it is that Mr Nicholson wants. Then we solve the problem.'

'I want those stones taken off the building.'

'That would set us back months,' Frye protested.

'They're dangerous. They have to go.'

'We've already agreed to cut all future slabs in half.'

Peter simply said what he knew: 'The ones already up there have to be cut too.'

'Impossible.'

'Somebody will be killed.'

'Nobody has so far.'

'Except Jerry Owen.'

'That was due to the crane touching the core structure.'

There was silence. Frye added furiously, 'If our suppliers had met their commitments, none of this would have happened.'

'But now it has,' Peter said.

Then Maifredi leaned forward. Smiling, his voice soft and gentle, he said to Peter, 'You know, I thought when you come today, you are just wanting to go to bed with my daughter again. Like yesterday, and the day before, no?'

Dick Frye swivelled his head quickly to exchange a glance with Thea, who was now standing very attractively in the middle of the room, brushing out her hair. There was not a trace of expression on her face. The Australian turned back and stared across the table.

Peter caught the exchange and found himself trembling. 'Were you invited to have a go too?' he asked. He had to clench his teeth to get the words out.

'Shut up!' Frye shouted. 'Okay? Just shut up.' There was a sudden violence about the man. 'You're in the shit up to your eyeballs, okay? We can get you fired any moment we want.'

'I want those stones taken off the building,' Peter repeated. 'They are very dangerous.'

Maifredi shook his head slowly, and at the same time leaned back even further on his chair as if to thrust his belly up at them. He spoke to Thea for a moment and she left the room. When Frye started to speak, Maifredi held up his hand, mouthed the word, Wait. The knitting needles clicked back and forth across the edge of this new silence. The woman hadn't looked up throughout. A mask of domesticity. Or as if she were knitting a great net she might in the end drop over all of them. The maid came in pushing a sweets trolley. Maifredi served himself from a gooey, brown and cream mass. When Peter opened his mouth, the older man again raised his hand. 'We wait for the last link in the pattern. Then we will have our symmetry. And everything is settled.'

Thea returned, slim, swaying, her red robe teasingly loose. She tossed a packet on to the table in front of Peter. The name Kodak on a black and yellow background, like the Fanta ad behind the plane on the beach and Donald Duck squawking in the local language this morning, took on a disturbing significance.

'Look at them.'

But Peter slipped the pack straight into his inside jacket pocket. No doubt his pleasure and fecklessness had been reified there in small rectangular snaps. Visibly shaking, he said, 'I don't doubt your ability as a photographer, Dr Maifredi. I presume that's the only way you can get it up.'

Thea swivelled round and in an instant was leaning across the table to slap him. As she had once before. Peter jerked his head back, almost falling from his seat. He was quite nauseous with adrenalin. Maifredi shouted at her. Drawing back, face flushed as it hadn't been in sex, the girl had to pull her robe across a breast that had slipped out.

'You ask yourself why I spoke of symmetry, Mr Nicholson . . .'

'Not at all,' Peter interrupted. 'What you're really talking about is blackmail. Speaking of which, you can have this.' He pulled out the envelope they had given Margaret on the beach. 'I never even counted it.'

'Then you're a fool,' Thea said, coldly.

'And impetuous,' Maifredi added. 'Symmetry, Mr Nicholson, is when things balance one to another and so . . .'

'Is this what he said to you people to get you to settle out of court?' Peter asked Frye.

The Australian said, 'Say what you mean, Maifredi, let's get this over with.'

'And so there is no movement,' Maifredi continued with evident enjoyment. 'Or there is movement frozen, as in art, round a vase.' He chuckled. 'We know too much about you, Mr Nicholson, and you about us. It is an embrace, a bond. You cannot say about us, and we cannot say about you. Otherwise we lose all equilibrium. We go down together.' He paused. 'If you make trouble, these photographs will be shown to your children, Mr Nicholson. Your little children, your wife, your lovely mistress.'

Frye's bony face showed signs of a relieved satisfaction. 'Clearer than that, Nicholson,' he said, 'you will not get.'

There was a silence as of men waiting for dust to clear after the plunger has been pushed.

'And Mrs Owen?' Peter finally asked.

'Mrs Owen is dead, Mr Nicholson. Your girlfriend telephoned for you here only minutes before you arrive to tell you the poor woman is found in the sea on the rocks.' He paused. His voice was soft and friendly, with always the assumption that the other would toe the line. 'This morning you saw her ghost. For that I am amazed. For that I am interested in you. The gods do not give to everybody to see ghosts.'

Peter pushed his chair back. 'I have to go,' he said.

'Do not be impatient, Mr Nicholson. I am sure that Thea is ready to take you back in an hour or so. We must still settle some details.'

'No, I'm going now.'

Standing up, swaying, he had a fleeting impression of the remarkable elegance of the room, the careful balancing of the various angles, the coolness of the marble floor, the way plants and vases complemented the underlying rectilinearity. Now he would have to walk out of this easy world into the intense afternoon light and heat.

'The stone,' Frye said sharply. 'We want the stone back.'

'Not to worry,' Maifredi chuckled. 'I think that Mr Nicholson has understood the situation.'

Peter turned. Thea was watching him. With more interest than he could remember. He said, 'The stone goes back to London with me where I shall be carrying out extensive tests. If immediate clarification is not given that all such stones are being removed from the façade, we shall be obliged to inform the Australian authorities.'

Another silence. When the sound of the knitting needles again rose to the surface, Maifredi suddenly screamed something in his own language, picked up a spoon and hurled it across the room at the woman. The clicking stopped and Peter walked free through the terrace windows.

Thea caught up with him as he hurried down the steps, past the pool. She took his arm. He shook it off. Barefoot, she stopped suddenly when they got to the limestone chippings. Peter kept walking. She started following him in the soil of a flowerbed. There was the slow hissing back and forth of a sprinkler.

'Peter! This is stupid. What are you trying to prove?'

She picked her way on clods and stones, shedding all elegance.

He kept walking. 'That I can't be pushed around.'

'But to what end? It's suicidal.'

Now he stopped and turned: 'To the end that I'm doing a simple duty. Making sure that no more of those stones fall on people. They have to be taken off.'

She caught up with him, just a few yards from her car by the gate. Breathless, wincing, discomposed, she was more attractive than ever. Because more human.

He asked, 'Anyway, why are you and your father supporting them so determinedly?'

'Now you're being naive.' She put her arms up round his neck and her wry smile had come back. She still believed she could seduce him. 'They owe us a lot of money. If they go bust so do we. Come on, I'm sure we can still settle this.' And she pressed her body against him through her robe.

He pushed her away. 'I'm doing my duty.' He repeated the words blindly.

Shaking her head, she said something in her own language. Something sad and mocking.

'What?'

'Goodbye, Peter.' She turned and was walking away.

'What did you say?'

Now it was she who kept walking.

He called after her. 'Listen, Thea, why don't you help me? You know I'm right. How can I not be? And we actually like each other.'

She stopped, turned. 'I'm not Medea,' she said, wryly.

He said, 'You could at least destroy the film to those photos.'

But there was no need, she said. No one would ever see them if he behaved sensibly. Changing her voice again, she asked from twenty feet away, 'Now shall I give Mr Nicholson a lift back to town? On that understanding? We could still make love at my place if you like.'

She was perfectly serious. Peter turned round and walked out of the gate.

———— • ————

It is said that the primary source of all the minerals and rocks on earth is chondritic meteorites, stony masses condensed from the gaseous nebula around our sun. So one enigma leads back to another, the ground beneath our feet to the light about our heads, if one can properly think in terms of above and below. So, at the end of the day, geology and all the other earth sciences are turned inside out and shaken off amongst the stars and planets, vertiginously imponderable, seductively named after gods forever absent, ciphers of our origins. The earth, the sun; and between those enigmas, here on the enamelled surface of things, the carefully constructed enclosures in which we must operate, the conveniently rendered surfaces and perpendicular walls, the spreading networks of relationships, scales of values. Peter had used the word 'duty'; one word in the vast, comforting system language was, the structure that embraced and expressed all others. Thea had replied in her own language, knowing he couldn't understand. Why had she done that, simply opposed a system he didn't understand to his own? With that sad, mocking tone. As if here he had arrived at the ultimate *non sequitur*. Peter stumbled over stones in the sun's blazing light, small figure in a huge landscape. At least he hadn't sold his soul merely for the lift into town.

Could he really have seen a ghost? Outside the geometric paradise Maifredi's wall encircled, the country was formless, a tangled sweep of Mediterranean scrub, heathers and gaunt maritime pine, occasional outcroppings of granite, a rubble of scree on the steeper slopes. Only the dark ribbon of the road insisted on contours, discovered direction in the valleys, Ariadne's thread leading back from the monster. But he hadn't killed the monster, far from it, nor had the princess offered to help.

What place could ghosts have in what was no more than a constant flux of materials? Were they an afterimage of the spirit? As when one saw a profile that was no longer there? Or some freak polarisation of the light that enabled you to perceive what was always there? The air perhaps was full of ghosts. As of radio waves. It was just . . .

Hazel was dead.

Peter stopped. The grey-green landscape trembled in the heat. Why was he thinking in these terms? Why was he forever casting about for analogies instead of dealing quickly and sensibly with the facts, forever chasing the kind of insubstantial profundities that preceded sleep. Or as though his mind were trapped in neutral and him furiously pressing the accelerator. Could Hazel really have committed suicide? Wouldn't she have chosen to do so in some way that compromised those she believed were responsible? All her talk of revenge. Not to mention the apparently genuine intention to be on the plane home: tickets bought, suitcases packed.

High up in the air a buzzard circled over the weathered slopes of this ancient uplift. The food he had eaten and this pitiless sun were making him ill. Plus the general malaise in the back of his mind that was Margaret's no this morning. Margaret had said no. No, no, no. Quite suddenly, he stopped, turned. Not a car had passed along the road in fifteen minutes. He looked out across the glare of vegetation and saw a tower squat on a distant hilltop, the same he had seen on his way to finishing plant and quarry, he thought, though from the other side presumably, the next valley. He stared and instinctively, as one choosing a decision he knows to be wrong, Peter struck out across the open country.

They imagined that now the rock was up there on the façade it would not fall. As it might very well not, for five, ten, twenty years. They imagined they could take their money and run. Or rather, live quite normally. He tripped on a stone. The soil was acidic and poorly consolidated. The vitreous dark green of myrtle bushes thrived in hollows. Why should he care for a death twenty years hence? Any more than he cared, or didn't care, that this or that large-scale project would surely lead to other deaths: the Channel Tunnel, some poorly conceived mine on the Indian subcontinent. Civilisation counted on its sacrifices. We were all implicated. Guilt was collective, indivisible. Every meat-eater was deft with the slaughterer's knife. Why did he arrogate responsibility to himself? How was it he had allowed himself to get into a position where his sense of self depended on this gesture of integrity?

He had shown none to his wife.

None to his mistress. Dear Margaret. She had said no.

Unless integrity were just a cover for escape.

There was a knot in his stomach now. Tight and tightening. Peter took off his jacket, felt in the pockets, transferred wallet and photos to his trousers, then merely discarded the thing amongst rocks and scrub. His office jacket. He opened his shirt at cuffs and neck and breathed deep. The air was warm and dry in his lungs. But it wasn't enough. The landscape quivered. He would faint perhaps. Suddenly he put his fingers in his throat, bent low and vomited.

Feeling a little better, he sat on a stone and took the photos from his pocket. They were so incongruous. Far more than any ghost. Ghosts you expected to have a face you knew, but not this cheap pornography. Here was his tongue at her breast, his rather weak profile. The wall mirror must have been two-way. Extraordinary that people did that. He didn't look beyond the fourth or fifth.

Extraordinary, too, that Maifredi had known to say he would send them to his children. Before wife or mistress. It was towards the children one felt ashamed. Towards the children one protested one's innocence. What if the first slab tumbled down on a child?

He dropped the photos in the grass. They wouldn't send them until they had tried at least once more. Some other lever. Probably they would never send them. They wanted to stop him, not to take revenge. In fact, it was surprising they weren't following him, to have him lead them back to the slab. He stood up and looked around. Maifredi's villa was lost behind a low ridge, likewise the road. He turned to attack the long slope up towards the tower.

An aeroplane traced a straight line across the sky, soundless, high above. On the ground Peter was forced to zigzag. There were clumps of gorse, boulders. Then he trod on a snake. It had seemed just any old, dry stick. Instead it twisted fiercely and bit at his trousers. His whole body tensed with shock. Already the creature was vanishing. Perhaps two feet long, it held its head high, a wave rippling down its body as though across still water. Peter pulled up his trouser leg, but the skin was unbroken. Looking up again, he had the impression the landscape had rearranged itself somehow, the tower was nearer, gathering the countryside. In the sky above, the jet-trail was already twisting and disintegrating in stratospheric winds. Tomorrow evening he could be in his own home with his wife and children. His own compartment. If that was what he wanted.

They had built it at the top of the highest hill for miles. Presumably for sending messages, defence. The brochure had said there were similar structures in similar stone in the north of Scotland. That old flair for doing the same thing everywhere: rectangular blocks, skilfully interlocking to form a circular shape, narrowing as it rose. Probably they had just picked up the rocks from the abundant scree all around. Fifteen hundred years wasn't so long ago, the landscape would have been much the same. The individual blocks were roughly hewn, but the effect was not inelegant. And it had risen higher once. Perhaps it had been a temple of sorts, gathered from the earth, pointed at the stars: the age-old hallucination of upright stone. Something to worship.

Peter ran his hand across the familiar surface of weathered granite, walking around the tower till he found a low aperture. It stank. A young man was stretched out with his head lying on a backpack. Amidst the stones that had fallen from the roof was a scatter of bright colours: Coke cans, the aluminium foil of biscuit wrappers wrested from another rock on another continent. A syringe was stabbed into the charred surface of a log where a fire had been. Eyes opened in a bearded face: 'Hi.'

Peter said nothing.

'You following the leylines, man?'

'No,' he said. He withdrew. And on the other side of the tower, the next valley opened up as though laid bare to possible messages. Stony hilltops, sparse vegetation thickening as it led down to a distant village. Neat rows of vines on the lower slopes seemed a net to catch falling rocks in. High above, opposite, his eye finally searched out a dark discontinuity, and the tiny, yellow horizontal of a derrick.

The vomit was acid in his mouth. He needed to drink something. Walking for three hours now in constant sunshine over rough ground after a sleepless night, he was close to passing out. Aware too of a deliberate masochism. He had ceased to think of the rock, the tall building on the other side of the globe, Maifredi's threats, Thea's charms. There was something rather superficial about all that. Its dilemmas were only a gilded web tossed over some deeper and darker problem, where the intellect couldn't easily penetrate, where the rocks ground against each other in a telluric gloom. Again and again, as he pushed across the dry bed of a stream, skirted a patch of gorse, picked his way through boulders, he tried to imagine his homecoming of the following evening: how he and Margaret would stand in the crowded gangway of the plane while everybody wrestled their bags from the overhead compartments, how they would go through passport control together, laugh over the old photographs, stand beside each other watching suitcases and backpacks creak round and round the baggage collection belt, how they might make some last lame joke about choosing the Nothing to Declare line at Customs, and then, immediately afterwards, what, two, three yards from the sliding door that channeled you through to the dull tiles of the arrivals lounge, they would split up, they would split up, because she had said no, after which he would . . .

But at this point his imagination failed him. Time and again. It didn't appear to be a question of choice, but as if, once separated out, that compound of himself, Anna, Mark and Sarah couldn't be put back together again, or at least not without the same conditions of heat and pressure that had originally formed it. He simply couldn't see his wife's expression, couldn't imagine what form their embrace might take.

And so back to the plane, the hostess, the airline food, little kisses over a whisky perhaps, leaning out of the window to see the Alps . . .

Would he have the stone slab with him? To test in London? In his suitcase, in the belly of the plane.

It hardly seemed important now, though he was crossing this countryside for that.

How the mind broke up in a whirl of observations, details, reflections: the extraordinary markings of a butterfly, not unlike some igneous rocks under the microscope, his worsening headache, an overgrown path he followed, then left, the distant mouth of the quarry, the buzz of a horsefly, Margaret, a lizard on the crusty surfaces of a boulder; and all the things he had seen this week, the grinding gangsaws, temples, lava slopes, faxes, polished surfaces, clustering crystals, stark shadows, patterned microfractures, all floating by before his throbbing eyes, the poorly sorted sediments of a week of fierce erosion.

Peter stumbled and fell. For a moment he lay face down in something thistle-like. Then became aware that the heavy beating of blood in his ears was in fact a truck. The vehicle rumbled down the quarry approach road, a huge block simply resting on the trailer, pinned down by its own tremendous weight. He noticed the parallel lines of the bore holes, the arrow indicating the direction of crystallisation. Four men were sitting behind, backs up against the block, smoking cigarettes.

Still lying where he had fallen, he looked at his watch and saw it was past six. An hour lost somewhere. With the sun still high and hot above the hillside. He got up. The approach road had been surfaced with rubble sorted from the quarry. Mica and quartz glittered in the stones. There were still three cars in the parking area beneath an exposed face. Forcing down his nausea, Peter reached the prefab site-office and pushed the door. No one. He crossed the moulded floor to the drinks machine, only to find he had no coins in his wallet. But there was a Turkish toilet, shower and wash-basin. He drank the water despite its brownish colour. The worries had cemented together at the back of his mind now, no longer an aggregate but solid rock, part of his inner landscape. Some change had taken place. Splashing water over his face and neck he experienced the immense relief of being reduced to basics: thirst, self-preservation.

———— • ————

A fly buzzed in the dust of a column of light. In the quarry manager's office Peter sat at a table where there was a small computer screen. The pornography was still there on the walls, a mimed sensuality, ghostly images from which the subjects had quickly stepped aside. He picked up the phone and dialled the hotel. Margaret was out. She had left no messages. A Mr Murray Davidson had asked him to be in touch as soon as possible.

Two men came into the room, overalls caked in dust, speaking their own language. One looked at him curiously, the other said something and they picked up bags and went out. Briefly, phone in hand, fingers on the touch-dial, Peter imagined contact with Murray, their voices mingling, their relationship. But it was not a side of himself he wished to expose. Everything would become too complicated. And it was positive that Margaret had been out. There was too much dispersion. In the bright light outside, a diesel began to throb.

Waiting, he switched on the computer. One menu led to another. Each block had an identification label, each identification label led to a document with 3-D graphics indicating dimensions, direction of crystallisation, date of extraction, optimum disposition on the gangsaw. It was more efficient than he had imagined. With a huge and utterly futile effort it would even be possible perhaps to bring back all the slabs from Australia and rearrange them in their exact positions in the quarry. Except that each time a slab was cut, more or less the equivalent amount was broken down into dust. And it was pure chance whether you turned out to be in the dust or the slab. There was no putting things back how they were.

The machine noise grew louder, then stopped abruptly. Peter noticed that the grimy window was finally free of direct sunlight. The flies in the room seemed lost, despondent. Three men came in, talking loudly, laughing; then the quarry manager. Again Peter immediately felt a certain affinity with this thickset man, as of one who recognises a friend and rival. He had sunglasses on, his neck smeared with sweat and dust, stout in green overalls.

'I am not expecting you,' he said. But wasn't unfriendly. 'You look . . .' his voice trailed off.

Peter was stained and crumpled, hair tousled, shirt filthy. He felt odd without his jacket. 'I'd like to talk to you,' he said.

'I am hurrying,' the manager said. But sat down. 'My wife,' he smiled. 'She is . . .' he cast about for a word, 'jealous.'

It crossed Peter's mind this was a stupid thing to say. The man pulled out a cigarette. Peter refused an offer, waited for the other to light up. Then enunciating very carefully, so that there should be no mistake, he said, 'Yesterday, I showed you a slab. A couple of hours later everything changed. Everything changed completely. Why?'

He was sure the other man felt the same affinity. They were two technicians embarrassed by politics and sub-terfuge, lacking any desire to manipulate, proud of doing simple, practical work. The quarry manager hesitated. 'If you have the questions, they must be more specific.'

Okay, Peter thought, then asked, 'Is it possible that I saw Mrs Owen alive at ten o'clock this morning? Yes or no?'

The quarryman was staring.

'Alive, walking around, not dead,' he insisted. 'About ten o'clock, ten thirty.' He could just see the other man's eyes through the dark, smeared lenses of his glasses. They told him nothing.

Peter waited. 'It's just that I have the impression that between the moment I showed you the slab and the moment I was told to go home there wasn't really enough time. I mean for two companies to decide to settle a big dispute out of court. Nowhere near enough. Then Mr Frye must already have been on his way from Australia, but nobody had told me about it. And that is extraordinary. Because he works for our client.'

The quarry manager shook his head. 'I cannot follow what you say. My job is to extract this rock from this hill.' He fidgeted on his seat. But he hadn't decided to leave yet.

'You saw the rock that killed that man,' Peter said, 'and I think you must have known what it was.'

'No,' the man said simply. 'No, I didn't.' He took his glasses off. The eyes were small and dark in a fine webbing of wrinkles. 'I did not know.'

'Okay, but when you told your boss, he knew. He already knew. Otherwise there wasn't enough time. And the moment he knew I had the slab, both he and the Australians wanted me to leave as soon as possible.'

'How can I say?'

'Please,' Peter said, 'please, tell me something useful.'

The man scratched in sweat-matted hair. He had spent the afternoon under a hot helmet. He smiled nervously. 'Mr Nicholson, last week I am told you are coming to look at the quarry. I am told it is a formality. I am told there is not need to make things look good, you know, to make things very ordered, like sometimes, when the client comes.' He paused. 'Then when you are come they tell me you are come with a girl. You are only interested in your girl.'

Peter breathed deeply. It was true Murray didn't usually let him do the foreign trips. It was true Marlborough Place was the senior partner's personal client. But he had put his lucky break down to the way things just couldn't seem to go wrong with Margaret, a sort of destiny that they would be able to get this time together. He asked, 'But was there anything to see? Something I missed.'

'Nothing. No really, nothing.'

'But . . .'

'Nothing. I know our method is old dated. The face is too, too . . .' He lifted his hands and brought them together to indicate narrowness. 'And there are many faults in this deposit. Also the phenocrystals are very, very big for job like this.' He shook his head. 'Nothing, nothing of very important. We cut good stone.'

Peter believed him. 'But Maifredi knew about the other rock?'

The other man shrugged his shoulders.

'I don't understand why I was sent here. I was told to find something at all costs. Now it seems everybody knew there was nothing to find. Even the Australians.'

The chubby man smiled and got to his feet. 'Better for you,' he said. He laughed. 'You have had the week with the girlfriend, eh? For doing nothing. I wish! It is for that perhaps they send you.'

Peter couldn't even smile.

The quarryman pulled a watch from his overalls pocket. He had to go. There was his dinner. Already cooking. His wife didn't like him to be late. He asked, 'You have a car here?'

Peter said he had left it a couple of hundred metres down the road.

They were perhaps twenty paces apart when the man stopped and called to him. He was leaning on a dusty white Golf scratching behind his neck. 'Mr Nicholson, okay, I have seen a stone like to that once. You know? The stone you bring here. I was at the finishing factory. But it was more than a year ago. I don't know if it is the same. They bring it from the continent and cut it for the Middle East. Just another job. I don't know if it is the same.' He turned and climbed into his car.

Day Five

Evening

Seven thirty. The hillside had come into sharp relief as the planet rolled away from the sunshine. Silhouetted, the old uplift was jagged and substantial, despite millennia of erosion dragging it back to a flat sea. Peter noticed how groundwater had scored channels across the quarry approach road. Summer storms perhaps, little spurts in the slow, downward creep towards peneplain. He would have enjoyed such a rain now. He and Margaret had walked a great deal in the rain, after office hours, or at lunchtime, when there was nowhere to go and they hadn't wanted to sit in pubs. Anna too, years ago. There was a photo of her cheerfully holding a red umbrella over his head as he hammered at Precambrian quartzite north of Aberdeen. Later she had come to hate the rain. Last year in the Lake District she had hardly left the cottage once. He had trudged with the children over Palaeozoic massif, told them of the Zechstein Sea and its retreat. Children loved to tread in puddles. They were still close to some pure source of energy, something undefined that might become anything. Near the well-spring, they hadn't collected their burden of sediment yet. They saw their reflection in muddy pools and stamped. The surface shattered. They giggled. They built pebble dams they knew would be washed away, castles of wet sand. Perhaps that was another reason why he had bought the earthquake puzzle. It had seemed more childlike than stately houses and gilded carriages.

Only lovers and children were happy to walk in the

rain. Later you learnt to defend yourself against its slow attrition. You bought houses and furniture, studied pension schemes.

What would become of the children without him? What had he done to them, or denied them? An unborn child to be taken walks through the rain? What would his absence mean? Peter quickened his step down the stony track.

Exhausted, he found himself thinking of kisses, Margaret's kisses, her low, soft voice that so entranced him over the phone. The office would disappear round about him. No wonder the others had noticed. All detail dissolved in her kisses. As though her saliva were some extraordinary solvent. The light in her dark eyes didn't reveal the world, but invited you to lose yourself in another. Stopping, looking up for a moment, he almost blacked out. And he sensed how love wasn't so much the simple extinction of self in sex, as the way in which one was led there: the unique path to a usual ecstasy. As life was valued not by whether one died early or late, but by all that brought you there. With Thea's perfect body he'd done no more than turn a switch on and off, life-death, life-death, as she had said, the numbing throb of a machine transfixing the continuum, on-off, on-off, back-forth, louder and louder, without individuality, the savage slabbing of the gangsaws grinding through stone, the blades rocking back and forth on their huge frame, the rhythmic spraying of steel shot in lime solution, louder and louder, deafening almost. For Christ's sake! Peter shook his head fiercely, afraid of madness, as a helicopter burst over the two-dimensional silhouette of the hill.

He stretched himself on the stones at the base of the embankment. Whether or not it was looking for him, he didn't want to be found. The machine passed overhead, whirling blades cleaving the sky. The racket was so loud one could neither think nor feel. A stream of air pressed him against the rock. Then it was gone. And at the next bend he just caught the gear change of a car in time to jump down and hide amongst the scree below the lip of the road. Thea and Frye were driving fast up to the quarry. He huddled still. For ten minutes, twenty. It wasn't an ordinary scree. It was too closely packed, the debris too regular in size, as though a stream of boulders led down the hill in some Brobdingnagian road. Studying the topography above and below, he guessed this must be part of a crude system of slides they had used to bring quarried stone down from the hilltop, sixty, seventy years ago, before the now-obvious truck had penetrated the rough terrain. They would have dragged the blocks over this packed rubble using a system of ropes, wooden rollers and winches. Nobody would have enquired too carefully into deaths occurring as a result of slithering blocks. It had been evident that if you wanted to win the rock and will it into some convenient shape, there was a price to be paid: donkeys dragged to their deaths in roped trains and limbs crushed under stone that was anyway brought out mainly for tombs and churches. Like the altar top he had seen on the island where he had almost spoken to Margaret. To say what? Make what sacrifice? Was there anything he could say to anybody that would change his life? Or perhaps he had changed it enough already.

The helicopter circled slowly above the hilltop higher up, then was gone again.

Peter chose not to get up from where he sat. He would wait for twilight to bleed into darkness. If he could nap in the meantime that might be useful. But his mind was uncannily clear. Though he suspected untrustworthy. It was racing too fast. And he wished he'd had his computer to martial thought in visible words and sentences. He always felt so authoritative when he detached his ideas from the flux his mind was and wrote them down. The quarry manager had wanted to help, but was conditioned by constraints of loyalty and fear. He had thus offered what amounted to no more than a single pebble, both hoping and not hoping that the geologist could reconstruct a whole terrain from that. What was that hidden landscape? The company had worked a similar stone for another project, this time in the Middle East. Climatic conditions *in situ*, at least in terms of wind factor and minimum temperatures, would have been less aggressive. Most probably the anchoring system was the traditional top-and-bottom ledges with backbolt. Demanding nothing special of the material. And the fact that the stone had come from the mainland was hardly surprising, given the huge capacity of the finishing plant. Clearly they couldn't always keep it supplied from their own quarries.

But what did any of this have to do with Marlborough Place?

And what did Marlborough Place have to do with Peter Nicholson? Nothing. Like some feckless gambler, his inability to leave the table was just his horror at returning home. To himself.

Or could he genuinely be doing it out of a sense of duty?

Or because Margaret had challenged him to act with integrity? Was he doing it to impress her? To win her?

But it didn't matter which. The fact was he had his excuse. He was tired, but not unhappy. At least the monster of routine was in the dust and writhing. Despite not having slept, when he got to his feet in the gathering dark, he felt refreshed.

———— ● ————

Imagining it would cross the road at various points, Peter started to slither down the scree slide where great masses of stone had once gone before him, pushed and restrained by armies of strong men. He thus mistook the first rumble of thunder for a possible rock fall. He huddled into a ball, arms meaninglessly protecting his head, not unlike a small figure the earthquake puzzle had ingeniously divided across four pieces. But nothing. Car headlights on the road above him quarried the landscape. Heat lightning found the profile of a ridge. Crickets whirred with machine-like monotony in the coarse grass amongst the stones.

He stood up and pushed on, gauging distances, trying to remember. Years of gravity and magnetic surveying had given him a good eye for landscape. He could read the movement of the hills, even guess what was on the other side. Would that people were so easy. At the bottom of the slide he crossed the quarry road, having saved himself a mile and more. Then the thunder again, as though a great sphere of granite were being rolled down a steel ramp. But no sign of rain. A sliver of moon beckoned in a cloudless sky, and a thousand stars invited him to find shapes and faces across unimaginable distances. He looked up and gazed. At the next bend, as expected, he found the slide again, the stones faintly white.

People. To calculate the Bouguer Anomaly, for example, you just took the extent to which gravity deviated from an established norm, discounted topographical and geographical factors, and anything remaining must be due to what was hidden beneath the ground: lightness where you expected density, or quite possibly vice versa. Something was going on: a different rock, a salt dome, a buried ridge. But could you do that with your wife, your boss? Discount social background, age, sex, class, environment, and any remaining idiosyncracy must be, well, them? Peter stumbled and fell. A fierce pain in his knee made him catch his breath. Certainly, he had misread Murray, despite having worked with him for nigh on six years. The company must be taking a kickback. And could any amount of surveying have told him how difficult Anna would become after their second child? Or what precious deposits were hidden behind Margaret's curiously asymmetrical features? A nerve stabbed. He had to sit down for a moment, roll up his trouser leg.

Streak lightning split a slab of sky, almost directly above his head. A line of cloud had materialised. The sudden thunder was deafening. The crickets were silenced. When the first drops of rain struck the rocks the descent promised to become treacherous.

He picked his way slowly. From the time spent in the car the other day, he reckoned a distance of three or four miles, though he was going cross country in the dark now, slithering over boulders in drenching rain, nursing a twisted knee. The stony ground chuckled with water and the air thickened with fresh summer dampness. In the event, he had to cross the road twice more, then heard the place before he saw it: first the base thump of the bladeframes, then the shrieking of tortured stone. He dropped over a small ridge and the noise swelled. He was coming down the hillside right above the deposit yard, protected, for no reason he could understand, by a six-foot wire fence, more a mentality, surely, than a useful investment, since even in the sad state he was in he climbed over it in no time at all.

The blocks formed a gridwork of aisles and islands, whitish in the wet dark. Four together, forming a square, each resting on wooden spacers and with half a metre or so between, so as to leave room for the lifting cradle. Then an aisle, then another four. Or sometimes more if the stones had been piled up, like children's building blocks, or totems. White lines criss-crossed the rocky ground. Each island had a code of letters and numbers.

Peter limped along cautiously. There were no shadows with the moon obscured, just glimmers when a light from the open lateral wall of the plant caught raindrops or surface water. He was decidedly cold now in just his wet shirt.

A figure detached itself from the darkness. He had picked up a stone for the purpose some minutes ago and raised his arm. Just in time her voice called 'Peter.'

——————— • ———————

All minerals are crystalline, but they do not necessarily occur as geometric crystals. All have the potential to display their orderly atomic structure in the smooth faces and symmetrical angles of prisms, pyramids and pinacoids. But nature is so abundant, so prone to redundancy. Little becomes what it might be. And even then identity can declare itself in different ways: allotropes of graphite or of diamond. So much depends on the environment, the pressure, the presence of water, the dynamics of heating and cooling. If Peter had ever been himself with Anna, with his job, with his children – and certainly he was nobody else – all the same it was a different, less splendid self from the one he had briefly discovered with Margaret. So that embracing her now in the discomfort of heavy rain and gritty wet clothes he was immediately exhilarated by the feeling of wholeness she gave him, of complete self confidence – it never failed to surprise him – and for a moment it seemed if only he could see this whole thing through, prove his integrity, his worthiness, then somehow, despite her no, he would have won the right to enjoy her transforming company for ever. But she said: 'I've got a car, Peter, let's get back to the hotel.'

She had a white silk scarf round soaking hair, a T-shirt clinging to breasts and shoulders. 'I guessed you would come here,' she said. 'I don't know why, but I knew.' Then she asked if he had heard Hazel Owen was dead? She had been invited to identify the body. It was horrible. Embracing her again, Peter asked, 'Did she have a ribbon round her neck?'

'What?' The body was so bruised and disfigured by sea and rocks. There was almost no face at all. 'Why do you ask?'

He shook his head. 'And Wendy?'

They hadn't found her. Margaret had half wondered whether she mightn't find her here too, come to the finishing plant somehow. Maybe she thought her mother had come here. 'Let's get in the car,' she said. 'Let's go. It's our last night. Today's been so horrible.'

Their last night. He had his back against a block. There were twenty yards of hard cement before the open wall of the factory where the gangsaws slabbed through the darkness on automatic. Rails protruded from the machines out across the cement so that the block trolleys could be wheeled into the yard to take their next load from the derricks. With the steady shrieking of the blades the lovers were obliged to put their lips to each other's ears.

He said, 'Look, I want to go in there, to the offices. There's just one last thing I need to find out.'

Her face, slightly below his own, was quizzical.

'Then we're going to go home and I'm going to beg you to live with me. Okay?'

She was silent. Distant lightning sparkled the rain on her cheeks. She said, 'Let's not talk about it now,' and she reached up to kiss him. Their lips met. There was that extraordinary feeling of slow dissolution. Breaking off was like the shock of waking. He stared at her. Presumably there had been and would be millions of girls like her: as there were millions of years, millions of mineral combinations in constant flux, that vertiginous abundance of everything. Yet once again he had the illusion nobody could ever combine so perfectly with himself.

If only the lots would come out of the urn in his favour. For two, three minutes then in the rain they enjoyed the pleasure of everything still to be sorted out, kissing, holding each other at arm's length, then embracing again, until she said, 'Peter, I haven't done anything with my life yet. I'm not ready. I don't want you to leave your family for me. It's too much.'

Margaret led the way back to the car. So that he would know where it was. They crossed a corner of open space and the pedestrian gate was open. A hundred yards away there was a narrow track through bushes. She had rented a Mercedes, of all things, on his hotel bill. That should have been worrying. Peter limped towards it, his knee fiercely stiff after standing still for a few minutes.

In the car they embraced again. Rain fell on the windscreen with a steady drumming, and occasional lightning found their outlines ever more intertwined. She seemed determined to make love to him, not to let him hurry off. Her gestures had that deliberation of a love which is quite sure of itself, despite the situation, despite his grimed, damp, sweat-stained shirt, despite what she had said only a moment before. They kissed in the isolated car, between the tall myrtles, a couple of hundred metres from the factory. They had made love in cars so often. They actually liked that vulnerability of something that might be discovered or harassed at any moment. That was the nature of their relationship. And it had always been easier than discussing some improbable future.

She pushed the seat back, unbuttoned his clothes, laughed when he told her about the jacket he'd thrown away. His office life, he said. As he could cast off all his past. He could. No, but she liked the fact that he was steady, staid, she said, 'Yet such a volcano beneath it.' She liked his disguise. She said, 'You're where the volcano comes out of the sea,' because they enjoyed saying things that made no sense. 'I loved you swimming,' he whispered.

'When you went under water and then came up and tossed your hair.' So red, and all the droplets sparkling off. Nothing but the sea behind. But now she found his bleeding knee. 'You poor thing!' She slipped off her headscarf and bound it tight round the wound.

They began to pleasure each other, laughing at the details of seat adjustment, breaths warm against the upholstery. And now their whispering began in earnest, that way they had learnt of making love as much with their voices as their bodies, mouths at each other's ears, encouraging, praising, worshipping, a rapidly rising temperature of language which would finally fuse obscenities, prayers, banalities, as if in the deep underground of their love there was no physical law that demanded these things be kept separate. Was this the miracle he had always been waiting for? This sense of being re-created, re-made, when everything had seemed shattered, when all kinds of dangers hung over them, this sandcastle endlessly to defend and rebuild together before a flooding tide.

Came the silence of afterwards. Fogged over, the windows ran with rain, then glowed with the light of passing headlights. They sat still. A car must be turning into the plant.

'The two supervisors changing shift?' It was midnight. Conjecture.

'Can't you just take the other slab back to London and test it there? That would be enough, surely.'

'And Wendy? You were so worried about her?'

She still was. But the girl had disappeared, she wasn't there to be looked after any more. Then her mother was dead. The police would find her and send her home. 'Why not just drive back?' she begged. 'Come on, Peter.'

So he explained about the other stone the quarryman had mentioned, for the Middle East. There was so much that didn't add up. This whole trip had been an elaborate front. But quite who was supposed to be fooled by it he didn't know.

She said of course it was important about the slabs on the building, but surely he only needed to inform some inspecting authority. Her face was shadowy and ill-defined in the dark light of the car and her voice all the more intense because of that. She was a bit afraid, she said. She had seen her first corpse today. Somebody she had spoken to only the day before. 'What if Hazel was pushed off the cliffs?'

'I thought of that.' Peter hesitated: 'They didn't actually say when she died. What time?'

'No.'

So then he explained why he had asked about the ribbon; he told her about the two figures staring out to sea, how he had feared his mind was breaking up and other worlds flooding through the cracks.

'Weird.' Margaret was nervous. In the dark of the rented car with heavy rain on the roof. She laughed uncertainly. 'Are there cases of ghosts travelling thousands of miles? Peter?'

But he said, probably it wasn't her at all. Just someone in a black dress scared of getting sunburnt.

'But you say you recognised her handbag.'

The posture of the body too, he said. The short, shaggily clipped hair. Then, in the way one does at last appreciate the obvious, he realised that it was seeing that figure on the beach that had really decided him to persist with this business. Looking out to sea, to that volcanic island, Hazel had been beckoning to him. And again when she had told the daughter to come to him, of all people. When she had given the slab with her husband's blood to him.

'Let's go, Peter. Please.'

He said, 'Look, I know where the office is. It shouldn't be too difficult. Give me an hour.' Turning back to the car, he had her open a window and added, 'Try and decide what suburb you want to live in.' Her eyes had the liquid black of the night itself. 'I love you, Margaret,' he said. 'I do love you.'

———— • ————

The dark, the falling rain, the incessant clamour of the machines: they seemed to have something in common, they were all elements that eluded distinction. But now Peter Nicholson would go in there and bring out the one detail that counted, that brought order out of confusion, mapped a landscape.

Water ran on the track between the bushes. Mud splashed on his ankles. His knee was stiff beneath the tight scarf. Not a ribbon for an athlete. He reached the point where the stony surface of the quarry road met the asphalt that brought cars and workers from town. A great mountain of granite saw-sludge loomed. There was the silhouette of the conveyors that brought it out from the factory. He stopped. Every shape and surface had to be seen in the glow of a single arc lamp above the car-park of the plant.

He hobbled in the windless rain, crossed the quarry road, went through the gate and reached the side of the plant that was open on to the deposit yard. Immediately the noise of the gangsaws penetrated his head, throbbing and wailing there, as if replacing thought. Without protection it was painful. The ears and mind were oppressed. He had to stop, make an effort to concentrate, to be himself.

The night-watchman would be in the foreman's soundproofed cabin, whence a sliver of light. Peter's hand slid along the parapet marking the danger area around a saw. The machine didn't need to see to cut those slabs to millimetric precision. There was only a faint glistening of dark metal. The huge drive wheel spun in its pit, the transmission piston converted rotation into the reciprocating motion of the bladeframe. Hydraulic tensers kept eight tons on each blade. And on its trolley, the block of stone was ghostly white, leucogranite, the scores of blades almost half-way through. Peter would have liked to look at the stone more closely, but once beyond the parapet there was the threat of tons of metal in rhythmic movement. Above the saw, a series of nozzles provided a constant stream of water, lime and grit, which collected in the pit beneath for filtering and recycling. A chip of stone flew off and ricocheted against a column. Under international norms the whole thing should have been covered up.

He walked quickly up the line of saws, then went off into the relative stillness of the trimming and drilling machines so as to circle the foreman's office. Only the saws worked at night. But touching an upright it was alive with vibration all the same. So much energy was being concentrated into such violent attrition. The cost of all those squares and right angles. His head sang. Then he was the other side of the plant by the door that led to the offices. It wasn't locked. He stepped through and let it swing and slam on its spring behind him. There was no danger of being heard.

Stairs led up a narrow well. Sound-proofing reduced the clamour to a low roar, as if a rushing river passed beneath the building. He felt his way through darkness, pushed a door. Night-light from a window opposite showed a few lab facilities, a petrographical microscope on a bench, clamps, frames and weights for simple mechanical tests, a drawing board. It might have been the scene of his dream almost twenty-four hours ago now. One dreamt more, of course, under pressure. And seeing those ghostly figures on the beach had been a sort of daytime dreaming. It meant no more than that.

Strain between the particles that were oneself. The truth was he was safely in a world of objects here. Notions such as evil in the rock were patently fanciful.

All the same, the sense of *déjà vu* as he switched on the light and walked over to the microscope was inescapable. A thin section of granite had been placed on the rotating stage. He hesitated. He bent forward, but was suddenly terrified that in daytime consciousness he might look into that eyepiece and see the man's face in mica and quartz: biotite the eyes, magnetite the wound. With no other world to wake up to. He bent down, fascinated by the instrument, suspecting for a moment that it had been left there on purpose for him. Then drew back sharply. This wasn't what he had come for. And how incredibly stupid to turn the light on! Looking up he saw his incongruous reflection in a great tombstone of polished black glass: the wet shirt, tousled hair, childish face. He moved quickly, snapped off the light, went out through the door, pulled it to and stood in the utter blackness of the corridor. The thing to do was to find a computer and coax out of it the information the quarry manager had hinted at: the cancellation of that Middle East order, the re-machining of an inferior stone for Marlborough Place.

He moved along, feeling for the doors in the dark. They must all be on the right, since the wall to his left divided the offices off from the plant. He turned a handle, pushed. But it took so long for things to declare themselves. He had to smell, touch, then eventually found a toilet roll. The next door gave out the staleness of stacked paper and cleaning equipment: a cubby. Glass in the wall a few paces further seemed to have a fire extinguisher behind. He should have brought a torch. Until, on pushing perhaps the penultimate door, a big window looked out over the car-park and the one arc lamp outside was enough to betray three desks, chairs, the usual office paraphernalia of blotters, typewriters, wall calendars.

An internal door presumably led to the last room in the line. He walked over to it, noticing that here where quality granite was abundant, they had paved the floor in cheap agglomerate. Perhaps all he had done in life was get himself into a position where he was paid for noticing such things. You traded in your ability to distinguish one matrix from another. Then found they didn't want you to see what wasn't convenient.

Still, he had arrived now. This was the manager's office. There were the comfortable indicators of framed pictures, a large, black, leather chair, the big, polished-wood desk. But, before sitting down at the computer, Peter crossed the room to check that the door to the corridor was unlocked. It was. And opposite, across the corridor, he caught the faint gleam of a handle. Another door.

It was like finding an extra element one didn't expect in some simple chemical formula. How could that be? A door giving directly on to the finishing plant? At this height. Why? A shadowy notice said something in that language he would never understand. The language Thea had replied in when he had used the word duty.

Peter crossed the corridor and turned the handle. The door was immensely heavy, because insulated he realised, almost a foot thick. As soon as he pushed it, the background noise swelled to a pounding clamour. Inside were perhaps three feet of empty space – that was the double wall – and then a second, smaller, metal door. This was bolted. He drew the bolts. The door opened awkwardly inwards, so that there was very little space between the two doors to squeeze past. Peter pushed through and found himself standing on the first section of the iron inspection walkway that crossed the entire plant just a foot or so above the gangsaws. Of course. There they were, thundering in the darkness below him, and, through the thick glass of the foreman's cabin not twenty yards away, pale light showed a man's legs crossed on a console, the cover of an open magazine. Peter withdrew quickly, and was just pushing the lower bolt into place when he noticed a tiny scrap of black cloth caught in the metal housing.

A moment later he was back in the manager's office. Again he looked at the computer. Again he found reason to delay. He went back into the main office, took a piece of headed paper from the typist's tray and found a biro. He wrote:

'Am in the offices of the finishing plant below the Palinu quarry (NB company paper). Midnight forty, July 18th/19th. Have just discovered Hazel Owen was here sometime the day or night before she died. Piece of black cloth certainly from her dress caught in the door leading from offices to inspection gangway over gangsaws. Only reason for going through there is she became trapped in the offices. Leaving offices via gangway means jumping approx fifteen feet to floor of plant. Or climbing down on to one of the blocks above the blades.'

Peter paused. The sudden violent back and forth of the bladeframe when she missed her footing would not have been unlike the crash of the sea against granite cliffs.

'Am going to look through company computer for information relative to unsafe stone on parts of Marlborough Place façade. Any discovery to be included in another fax before leaving this office. This in the event of something happening to me.

'PETER NICHOLSON.'

If only the police had listed fax numbers. Some 999 for such situations. If he sent it to Anna she would have a nervous breakdown. He decided on his own office back in London and punched out the number. The company name appeared in liquid crystal. The machine hummed, transferring his nervous scribble through two thousand miles of cable. He stared at it, wondering about Murray, his insistence on the phone this morning. No, he should spread the load, establish a sort of safety net . . . He called the hotel, got their fax number and sent another copy with Margaret's name blocked in on top. Which would have to do.

———— • ————

It was Cadmus the Phoenician first laid out a town whose geometric design was to correspond to the heavens. This was the same Cadmus who brought the letters of the alphabet to Greece. He took different-coloured stones from mounts Cithaeron, Helicon and Theumesus and piled them up to represent the planets. Later, the implacable Dionysus expelled him from his beautifully ordered Thebes, then destroyed the city with an earthquake. But it was not until Oedipus, the puzzle-solver and measurer, that a hero actually killed by mistake. As though, obsessed by his own measurements, this most lucid of men became blind to all else. Imposing order, he failed to recognise his father. Or was there some perverse underlying principle, first with Cadmus, then far more viciously with Oedipus, by which the smarter a man became with his set square, the worse his luck when the lots were cast from the urn? Some vendetta of identical Nemeses, or isostatic redressing of balances? Peter made his calculations so rapidly, so intelligently, when he finally found the file he was after: the surface area of the order, the size of the slabs, the feasibility of reworking. Crucially, the width was the same, the fixing method traditional, leaving the stone intact, accommodating a relatively modest modulus of rupture. And the destination of the order was Kuwait, with delivery in just two stages: the first to arrive on 1st August 1990, the second only a month later. So that by the time the Iraqi invasion took place the company would already have been dispatching the first shipment and have taken delivery of blocks for the second. Which meant a considerable amount of unsellable stone on their hands at precisely the moment the world market collapsed, precisely the moment, if he remembered rightly, when Marlborough Place had begun to reject large quantities of mostly reasonable if not ideal stone, whose microfractures they wrongly believed were treacherous.

Peter went through the specifications again. It all hung together. And this was so satisfying, he began to feel very excited and clever. Now all that remained was to sort out who, on the Australian side, had been a party to the decision to use this inferior stone, and who, after Owen's death and the expensive ensuing delay, had had to be hoodwinked with a pretence of claims against the supplier. Claims that were meant to fail, but would presumably serve the purpose of demonstrating good faith to someone else. A battle between contractor and proprietor? Or corruption inside the contracting company itself. Frye? Somebody had been so sure of themselves as to order that Peter stay on the island a whole week, convinced he would find nothing, would produce a report that offered no more than grumbles about microfractures and shoddy workmanship, which then some other expert would rightly demonstrate were unimportant. And when Maifredi phoned the proprietor to protest about his visit? Was that no more than an elaborate ploy to convince the proprietor that the contractor's investigation was being carried out seriously, to draw attention away from the stone that already clad five floors, stone that had perhaps saved the contractor from paying some crippling late completion fine? The thing to do was to find the appropriate telex roll. September, October 1990. Something like that. So it was that Peter got up from the screen and saw the little girl standing in the doorway.

For a moment he imagined he must be hallucinating. Or seeing another ghost. She was so wet and dishevelled, so ghastly in the green computer light.

'I thought Mummy would be here,' she said, calmly.

He had to sit down again. One knee was screaming with pain and the other simply gave. He shook his head. 'You terrified me.'

She laughed. 'Why?'

'I thought I was alone.'

'I've been watching you. You were busy.'

'Aren't you freezing?'

'No. The rain is quite warm.'

'You scared everybody by disappearing.'

'I thought Mummy must be here. I thought it would be easier for me to come than you or the police. I'm going to make her go home.'

He took a breath, then didn't have the courage. Everything was so strange in this grey-green light.

'How on earth did you get here?'

'Walked. I've been here with Mummy twice.'

'And nobody saw you?'

'I go invisible when I hold my jade.'

He stared at her. All she had was her white blouse and pink skirt clinging to a body thin as his own daughter's.

'Look, go back outside, go to Margaret in the car.' He explained how to find the place. 'Tell her I'll be out in another half hour or so.'

'Why don't I stay with you?'

'I've been much longer than I said I would be. If you don't go and tell her, she'll come up here too.'

The girl didn't move. He stood up, leaving the computer screen on for light. Probably the telex rolls would be in the secretary's room.

'You're not going?'

She shook her head. Then stepped aside to let him through the door into the main office. He would have to hurry. He began to open cupboards in the half-dark, pulling at the drawers of filing cabinets. The girl sat on a desk, watching him, swinging her legs. Until, without meaning to, he asked, 'Did your father have a tattoo on his arm?' At the same moment he found a drawerful of telex rolls.

'No. Why?'

His relief was so considerable he didn't even try to answer. He had merely seen two strangers on the beach. Now he was merely looking through a few telexes before flying back home tomorrow.

She laughed. 'But he used to say the scar on his arm looked like a bird. He'd got it trapped in something once. He said it tingled if I kissed it.'

Peter closed his eyes. The fuzz of light behind the lids gave him the impression of strangenesses and familiarities converging.

He turned. 'Your mother is dead,' he said. 'She fell off a cliff about five miles from here.'

The girl sat quite still, staring in the half-light.

'Look, I know it must be awful, I shouldn't have told you just like that, but please, go back down to Margaret and I'll be along soon and we can arrange for you to go home.'

'You're saying Mummy killed herself?'

'It seems so.'

Slowly the girl was shaking her head. 'No, no, she wouldn't have done that. Mummy wouldn't. She wouldn't. She said she was going to blow them all up. She never said . . .'

There was a sudden sharp whirring and the computer screen in the next room went dead. The arc lamp outside faded to an ember and was lost. For a moment he imagined a power cut, then realised he could still feel the faint throbbing of the gangsaws.

He found the girl by her paleness in the dark, grabbed her hand and pulled her to where the door to the manager's office was hardening in the shadows. They banged into a low cabinet. Then round and behind the big desk. He sat her on the floor and crouched beside.

Nothing. His ears strained. Just the drumming of the machines, the sound of engines in a ship. The stone floor was cold. Dust and polish. A smell of stacked paper, stale cigar smoke.

'Listen hard,' he told her. Her small body was trembling beside his. They held hands. The passing seconds seemed as long now as they had been brief an hour before in the car. Nothing. Perhaps it really was some sort of power cut. The supplies were different.

He whispered, 'She told you that?'

'What?'

'About wanting to blow up something.'

The little girl was silent. Around them the dark betrayed different densities: the desk, the space above, a sort of lacquering where a cupboard might be. Moving a little to ease the pressure on his knee, he upset a wastepaper basket and something rolled out, a can it seemed, clattering across the floor, alerting a web of nerves right through his body.

The girl drew in a sharp breath.

'Shush!'

The can rolled against something and was silent. He froze and waited. Perhaps in a moment they could get up. Meantime he said, 'Look, explosives are hard to find and complicated. She could never have done anything like that. She was just being melodramatic. Probably when she realised that she just gave up. She felt desperate.'

The girl shook her head. Her urgent child's whisper reminded him of games of hide and seek with his own children in the dark of their Barnet house. 'Do you remember when she ran to the quarry that morning, when we first saw you, and everybody ran after her in case she got killed.'

'Yes.'

'I took one of the boxes from the back of the van while no one was looking. She told me to.'

'What?'

'That they use to blow up the rock. Then she put it in her big handbag.'

The handbag she had rummaged in so carelessly the following morning at breakfast. He remembered the small manual amongst the mess of her papers, Use of BRG Pentaerythritol . . .

'Mummy's a bit crazy,' she whispered.

There was a sound of footsteps, perhaps on the stairs, a murmur of voices. Peter stiffened. They must have spotted the glow from the screen through the window and blacked out the lights immediately to cut off his source of information. Perhaps they had been waiting at the bottom of the stairs to see if he came down. Putting his mouth right by the girl's warm ear, he said, 'When the moment comes, I'll run off through that door. I'll make a bit of noise. They will follow. You run back the way you came and go to Margaret. Remember, through the gate, back towards the road. It's a track on the left.'

The steps had stopped in the corridor. The voices were incomprehensible with the dull rhythm of the saws. But a flicker of torchlight suddenly gave the door profile, then was gone.

'There's a telegraph post, too,' he said. 'Right at the corner.'

The girl whispered, 'It's okay, I saw you there before.'

'Before when?'

'When you were kissing in the car.'

He turned and saw the pale, unformed face. Every time he imagined he had separated something off in a compart-

ment of its own, it turned out everybody knew. The
mixture was explosive. He shook his head. Through the
dark, Thea's voice called, 'Peter. We know you must be
in one of these rooms. Please come out so we can talk
about it all in a sensible way.'

Again the torchlight along the corridor made a frame
of the doorway. But they were staying near the stairs in
case he was hiding in one of the rooms there. They didn't
want him to slip out behind their backs.

'Count to ten, then go.'

He got up, deliberately clattering the wastebasket,
went through the door that led directly to the corridor,
crossed it, was caught for a second in the beam of a
powerful torch, then heaved open the insulated door
opposite. Immediately they came running. 'Nicholson!'
It was Frye's voice. 'Hang about, we've got a better deal
for you. Something you can agree to.'

Peter got the heavy door closed behind him and fought
with the bolts of the other in complete darkness, jamming
his body back against the first door which they were
already trying to open. Then he was out on the gangway
in a gale of noise just in time to see the girl's slim figure
slip through the door almost directly below and melt away
into the dark rain beyond the saws.

———— • ————

Just a tiny jogging of the memory and it often seems
we might remember all our origins and everything that
is: if only we had some small key to help us, a clue
thrust into our hands as we grope about in a moment
of waking, or clutch at a smell that conjures a forgotten
landscape and is gone. Glancing up into the huge dark
of the plant, Peter knew he had been here before, was
on the edge of something, as one standing by the shore
at night often feels he is remembering other seas.

Or perhaps the truth of the matter was that he had been standing on this inspection gangway the whole trip, above the thunder of these machines which crushed thought, which sliced the hills to polished façade, and which held a curious fascination for him, not unlike the call of crashing surf, or the vertigo of cliff-tops, or sudden Siren sex. Perhaps, without realising it, both inspected and inspecting, he had been doing nothing more all week than pace this narrow gangway and look down into the mechanics of that prodigious demolition, the urge to jump growing ever stronger.

There were festoons of cables draped in the dark, a gridwork of rusting angle iron above his head. Dusty air streamed towards a filter. So that when you remembered the four nights of lost sleep, and the pressure from every side, of pleasure, pain, memories, fears, plans – his wife, his boss, his mistress, Hazel, Thea, Maifredi – then it was a small mechanical miracle he was still in one piece at all, not to mention thinking, acting, in the midst of this battering noise that swept across the mind like great breakers on the beach, bearing away all the day's sun-drenched intricacies: faces in the sand, footprints, and holes where children buried their fathers for fun. If only he had had time to send the second fax. That would have pierced this obliterating back and forth. Or if he had known a number for the police. But he wasn't beaten yet. Even as he glimpsed the girl escaping beneath, he had the sense to turn back and thrust the metal door hard inwards so that it jammed tight against the other, heavier door in the narrow space between the walls. They couldn't open it more than a couple of inches now. Peter stood wedged in the threshold, back to the frame, feet jamming the door, knee forced painfully straight.

'Nicholson,' he could barely hear Frye's shout. 'Have you gone mad, or what?'

He didn't answer. It was a question of time. Looking down he watched the oscillating motion of the bladeframe right beneath him, almost at the bottom of its block, the slabs standing together in parallel lines of white and dark. There was the pressure of a shoulder against the door.

'We've got an offer to make,' Thea shouted. 'We don't mean you any harm.'

Still keeping legs and back tense to jam the door, he cupped his hands and leaned forward. 'Is that what you said to Hazel Owen, before you pushed her down on to the saws?'

There was a pause. He could see the small neon glow in the foreman's cabin. Perhaps illuminating a pornographic magazine. It was curious that such monstrous machines should need their human guardian. In only a centimetre or so the blades on the first saw immediately below him would be through and the frame would hit its trip-switch, the stone severed.

Thea's voice called.

'Can't hear a fucking thing,' he shouted.

'You're right she died here. But nobody killed her. Now will you please open this door and let us talk to you.'

How long would it take the little girl to find Margaret? And what would Margaret decide to do? To go for the police would take at least an hour. Yet he felt more excited than scared. And immensely pleased with himself.

'She just happened to be dead, did she?'

'The foreman found her in the early hours. She had gone too close to one of the machines. You can ask him if you like.'

Their voices were screaming through the gap where one door jammed the other. The metal frame digging into Peter's back vibrated with the back and forth of the nearest saw.

'So why the cliff?'

But suddenly the almost obvious occurred to him. Simply, a revelation. And a lure. His mind was elsewhere. Thea's reply was lost.

Frye shouted, 'Listen, we're ready to do something about those panels, if you want to talk about it. Don't be ridiculous.'

His eyes were searching the thundering gloom, the great volumes of steel racing in the dark. Why hadn't he thought of this before? For she had come here of course, not to find anything but to carry out her revenge, which was also her inability to live with herself for some reason, some barrier she was up against. He could understand that. The grey return to a passionless life that haunted both of them. That was what brought them together. And she had known something might happen when she came, she had warned her daughter. Though in at least part of her mind she had expected to be on the flight back home the following afternoon. The suitcases had been packed, the bookings confirmed. The little girl was just waiting to go.

Frye screamed, 'We're willing to take those slabs off, if you play ball. Give us a year. Once the building's already officially delivered and the rent's coming in. We'll do them one by one. Maintenance.'

It was like trying to remember an elusive dream, with the fury of the gangsaws throwing up every possible resistance. His nightmare of two nights before, perhaps, that had cast him up into the waking world like some fragment of volcanic ash, forever ignorant of the explosion that had produced it, yet in its very structure telling all. He remembered walking to the window, the clamour of the street-cleaning machine catching the kerb, teasing memory, and then as he held up the fatal stone, a burst of sunlight sparking colours from its grey surface. What could have caused the explosion? Pentaerythritol tetranitrate didn't detonate any lower than two hundred degrees.

'We'll put some kind of vacuum diaphragm on the back. Okay?' Frye was shouting himself hoarse. 'For Christ's sake Nicholson, come out of there so we can talk. We need your opinion. We can sort this out. Nobody's going to hurt anybody.'

Unless under enormous percussion. He was staring at where the grid of cables and angle iron was slowly declaring itself in the void. The machines thundered. But how could a woman with no technical training have managed that? Staged a detonation? Not to mention inventing a time switch that would allow her to get on the plane the following afternoon, more than twelve hours after setting the thing up.

The sound of twenty bladeframes seemed to paralyse thought inside his head, prevent him from reaching the obvious conclusion. Some perfectly normal calculation was refusing to come out. The way his whole life at the moment seemed at once banal in its known quantities of wife, mistress, children, yet refused to resolve itself in any equation. He was stuck. The noise hammered and hammered at where he had jammed himself in the door frame. At least the nearest saw would be stopping any moment now.

With which thought at last he understood.

'All we want you to do is to hold off telling the authorities for the moment. Otherwise, we're bankrupt.'

'Get these machines turned off!' Peter screamed.

'We'll give you the negatives of the photos.' Thea's voice was barely audible. 'That was a bad joke in the end.'

'I said get these machines turned off.'

'Why don't you just come out? We can talk here.'

But Peter had already left the door. He was lost in the clamour of the noise. He leaned out over the gangway into dark space. The machine shrieked. Hard to tell, but the block was surely at its last centimetre or so. How long could it have been on that frame with an advance speed of, what, eight centimetres an hour? The luminous slabs rose at least two metres above the back and forth of the blades. They must have set it up the previous evening.

Then, as Frye and Thea realised the door was free and came out on to the gangway, Peter looked down to glimpse two other figures hurrying in from the deposit yard. There was the distant pearl of Margaret's face in neon and shadow, the little girl's rag doll frame.

He began to scream. It was all clear now: the nightmares, his sense of vertigo, the interminable calculations, the way one thing had stealthily been transformed into another without his even noticing. Above all there was the terrible seduction of it all, the fascination of such a complex mechanism, which only now revealed itself as a trap. Yet still so much more attractive than the sedimentary life he must otherwise return to.

He climbed the barrier. Mistaking the open mouth, soundless in the battering noise, for a cry for help, Margaret and Wendy were moving quickly towards him across the factory floor. Desperately he waved them away, standing outside the guardrail now, looking for the safest place to jump down.

Frye tried to grab him. 'You're crazy. You'll be killed.'

He dropped on to the machine.

Margaret froze, perhaps four or five yards away. He had a very clear vision of her slimness and fright, then had to leap sharply away from the course of the blade frame. 'Run!' he screamed. The sudden pause in tension as the drive rod changed direction had him off balance, but like a child dashing the last few paces of a slope, he hopped along a thin beam across the top of the structure and threw himself twelve feet to the factory floor. Pain flooded up from his knee. His head banged against the cement base. The air was sharp with a wet spray of lime and grit. As if he had jumped directly into a dream where sense, sound and colour were fused in some supreme apprehension of calamity. And yet, as so often in his dreams, there was still a part of him that could think with the quiet lucidity of heroes past, could think that this was foolish, that there was no need for it, that there must be a cut-out switch on some console somewhere, if only he had the sense to stand up and look for it.

But now Margaret was so close – no time even to tell her to leave – Margaret who had brought him to this, been herself a kind of explosion mining the dull terrain of his routine, Margaret who would never live with him, as he would never say those destructive words to his wife, to his family. He had appreciated that all along, even in his most earnest proposing and fantasising; he had always known it would never happen, that that was not how the equation came out.

Rolling on his back to push close to the block, he glimpsed the perfect round of Thea's face hanging over the gangway. Then Frye's shadow was hustling her away.

He could just get his hand between the grid of the trolley and the last uncut millimetres of the block which rested on four beams of wood defining three narrow cavities. Above, the thin slabs rose vertical on their way to perfect uniformity.

He forced his elbow in, face drenched in a fierce spray of water and lime. The monster was upon him now, the shrieking blades only inches away. When they came through the stone, they would slam down into the wood and hit the trip-switch.

Where was Margaret? Had Wendy understood and pulled her back. What a stupid revenge this was! How completely futile and meaningless, to take it out on these blind machines. Unless it was supposed to be some kind of passport to the inevitable afterwards, a gesture that would free her mind. His fingers groped. But there was nothing in this cavity. He wriggled his hand out. The blades were almost through. They were her detonator. He should get up and run. Maifredi's vase had been there to tell him that. 'I saw, let's run.' But he knew he was here because he wanted to be.

He forced his arm into the second cavity. Yes, yes, here was the sodden cardboard, a great wad of it. Done it. Pull it free. It was no more than wedged there. Harmless till the weight came down. And then there was a light too, a light that might have been the same sunshine he had been averting his eyes from all week, an intensity beyond imagination, not revealing detail, or not at this proximity, but hiding everything in its destructive brilliance: the shattering slabs, the chunks of steel and cement, the sudden prodigious expansion of a single point in a huge explosion of energy, instantaneous volume of gas beside which no bonds could hold, not the crystal lattice in the rock, not the cast-iron of the gangsaw, nor the concrete aggregate of its base. Least of all the blood and bone of a body reaching into the heart of that light.

Then the extinction, the clatter of falling fragments, a great boiling of dust, as if a curtain were raised over a change of scene, while behind it the particles, dreadfully metamorphosed, settled in their new, if temporary homes: the mangled drive wheel flung out into the deposit yard, a blade wedged in the shattered roof, splinters of grey rock, a severed leg bound with a headscarf lying on the polishing conveyor. And as the dust settled, all the pieces were still there for the finding, even if blood might have steamed off into the air, flesh and brain melted into scum. No, it could all be identified, the teeth (one of them chipped) numbered and compared with records, the fragments of bone collected in a handsome box. Only consciousness had vanished beyond the clutches and calibrations of any science. A consciousness unavailable in any photograph and only partially expressed in old letters, a consciousness indifferently, if intensely, recalled in the mind of a pretty red-haired young woman who, arm in a sling, would hurry through the Arrivals gate at Gatwick the following afternoon, unaware of another woman behind the rail who caught her eyes for just a moment, and who would harbour quite different memories. None of them Peter Nicholson.

EW

1	31	61	91	121	151	181	211	241	271	301	331
2	32	62	92	122	152	182	212	242	272	302	332
3	33	63	93	123	153	183	213	243	273	303	333
4	34	64	94	124	154	184	214	244	274	304	334
5	35	65	95	125	155	185	215	245	275	305	335
6	36	66	96	126	156	186	216	245	276	306	336
7	37	67	97	127	157	187	217	247	277	307	337
8	38	68	98	128	158	188	218	248	278	308	338
9	39	69	99	129	159	189	219	249	279	309	339
10	40	70	100	130	160	180	220	250	280	310	340
11	41	71	101	131	161	191	221	251	281	311	341
12	42	72	102	132	162	192	222	252	282	312	342
13	43	73	103	133	163	193	223	253	283	313	343
14	44	74	104	134	164	194	224	254	284	314	344
15	45	75	105	135	165	195	225	255	285	315	345
16	46	76	106	136	166	196	226	256	286	316	346
17	47	77	107	137	167	197	227	257	287	317	347
18	48	78	108	138	168	198	228	258	288	318	348
19	49	79	109	139	169	199	229	259	289	319	349
20	50	80	110	140	170	200	230	260	290	320	350
21	51	81	111	141	171	201	231	261	291	321	351
22	52	82	112	142	172	202	232	262	292	322	352
23	53	83	113	143	173	203	233	263	293	323	353
24	54	84	114	144	174	204	234	264	294	324	354
25	55	85	115	145	175	205	235	265	295	325	355
26	56	86	116	146	176	206	236	266	296	326	356
27	57	87	117	147	177	207	237	267	297	327	357
28	58	88	118	148	178	208	238	268	298	328	358
29	59	89	119	149	179	209	239	269	299	329	359
30	60	90	120	150	180	210	240	270	300	330	360